"In this novel inspired by the challenging life of the author's grandmother, a woman is left to raise her four children alone during the 1920s... Smooth-flowing prose carries the tale forward at a steady pace...farm and city vignettes create vivid images of time, place, and economic class, and Augusta emerges as a formidable woman in the face of daunting odds. A historically evocative period drama that's poignant and disquieting."

—*Kirkus Reviews*

"*Augusta* is an insight to another era and a testimony to a woman who became more resilient as she was challenged. Engaging writing propels the story through the decades of Augusta's life, and what a life it was."

—Jennifer Belton, former White House Library director

"Celia Ryker's latest book draws the reader in from the first pages, and allows us to follow Augusta's journey from a child bride in the Ozarks to a grown woman faced with the challenges of poverty and abuse. This true story comes alive with vivid characters and settings, so that we are immersed in Augusta's life as if we are there with her. The book honors the author's grandmother's perseverance and tenaciousness, and while it is a tale of the past, it has relevance today. Faced with difficult choices at every turn, Augusta shows that the human spirit has no bounds when it comes to a mother's love for her children."

—Anne Richter Arnold, journalist & writer

"Celia Ryker's newest book, *Augusta*, is a novel based on a true story chronicling a teenaged mother's fight to keep her family together through pre-Depression-era challenges that arise as she emigrates from a failed Arkansas farm to a Detroit tenement. An unspeakable decision, the circumstances leading to it, and the consequences of that decision drive the plot and make this book a page-turner.

Ryker's book evokes John Steinbeck's *Grapes of Wrath*. It is a beautifully crafted narrative detailing the trials of a girl married off to her best friend's father at the age of thirteen who finds herself abandoned and tasked with raising her family alone on the money she makes as a waitress. Augusta puts a smile on her face, presses through the cold-shoulder treatment she finds in Detroit and manages to create a support-community.

Life sends one challenge after the other, but through it all Augusta's determination stands as a beacon of hope. The ending brings the reader full circle from youthful dreams to marital realities and finally to the main character's self-actualization as a mother who needs to forgive herself in order to find redemption. This is a must-read for anyone interested in historical narratives, women's studies, or tales of true grit."

—Jennifer Falvey, *The Vermont Standard*

Augusta

Augusta

A Novel
Based on a true story

Celia Ryker

Rootstock Publishing

Montpelier, VT

First Printing: January 2023

Augusta, Copyright © 2022 by Celia Ryker

Release Date: 01/03/23

Softcover ISBN: 978-1-57869-120-3
Hardcover ISBN: 978-1-57869-835-6
eBook ISBN: 978-1-57869-121-0

Library of Congress Control Number: 2022912634

Published by Rootstock Publishing
an imprint of Multicultural Media, Inc.
27 Main Street, Suite 6
Montpelier, VT 05602 USA

www.rootstockpublishing.com

info@rootstockpublishing.com

Interior and cover design by Eddie Vincent, ENC Graphic Services (ed.vincent@encirclepub.com)

Cover Art: Daguerreotype portrait of Augusta courtesy of the author;

Photo of The Guardian building at night in the 1930s courtesy of the Detroit News Photographs, Walter P. Reuther Library, Wayne State University.

Author photo by Steven Nikola

For permissions or to schedule an author interview, contact the author at celia@celiaryker.com.

Printed in the USA

To Gramma Dawson.
She lived in a cottage on the lake,
taught me to appreciate a walk in the woods
and not to be afraid of loon calls or snakes.
Her life seemed wonderfully simple.
I didn't know then that
Gramma's name was Augusta.

Prologue

The round toes of her sensible shoes were barely visible among the fallen leaves. The sidewalk beneath autumn's litter was smooth and level, but her pace slowed as she neared the backyard on the corner. Her thin gray coat ruffled in a gust of wind, its mismatched buttons barely holding it in place. *Will she be outside? Will I get to see her face? If she's indoors I'll just walk on by, like so many other times.* Thoughts whirled through Augusta's mind as she neared her destination.

She was glad the sidewalks were empty. It was no secret she used to have four children and now had only three, but people who knew her story never spoke of it. She was ashamed of what she'd done, but, as a farmer's daughter, she'd learned early on about the harshness of life. It hadn't felt like she had a choice, even as she made it.

A waitress raising four children on her own, in 1920s Detroit, was but one of many sad stories. A regular customer had heard of Augusta's situation, and they had become friends, or at least friendly. Over the course of many meals they got to know one another, though they never sat down together. They chatted as Augusta brought sandwiches and soup, and Judith always left a healthy tip.

Augusta told family and friends when Ottis left. She'd thought her husband might have gone back to Alton, Illinois. He'd talked about that town like it was a slice of heaven, and had chosen Alton for his son's middle name. Augusta contacted people in Illinois she'd heard Ottis mention, but they denied knowing where he was.

She was afraid her children would end up in an orphanage, all of them. She'd had to work to feed them all, which left them home alone. The two older girls, Ivon and Thelma, twelve and thirteen years old, looked after their little brother, Buddy, and the baby. Sometimes, exhausted at the end of a workday, Augusta watched her daughters deftly changing diapers and wished their lives were easier. She could provide care or she could provide food, but it seemed impossible to provide both.

Lottie was an infant when her father walked out of their lives, young enough to perhaps be unharmed by an adoption. It wasn't clear to Augusta exactly how she'd let it happen. Judith and her husband had always wanted children, but after many years they'd given up trying. They promised to love and care for Charlotte. They could give her a good life and would provide money for Augusta to care for her family, what was left of it.

Augusta strained to remember how the question had been asked. *We were friends. No, we were never friends, we exchanged friendly words. I said too much and heard more than I should, feeling sympathy for someone who had so much more than I'd ever have. Sympathy sailed both ways in those conversations and now, since the adoption, we rarely speak.*

She shuffled through the leaves, hoping to see her little girl in someone else's backyard. *There she is. She's wearing a white pinafore I could never afford. She looks happy and healthy, but what could I do if she wasn't? I couldn't pick her up and take her home. And what if I did? What if I reached over that fence and hugged my sweet Lottie to my chest and ran away with her? I can't do that. I can only glance over as I walk by, like any stranger on any sidewalk, and hope to hear her laugh.*

The little girl in the perfect pinafore jumped up from her toys and toddled toward the sidewalk.

I know I shouldn't be here, but I can't stay away. Lottie has seen me too many times and her voice pierces me.

"Hi."

Augusta ignored her, her throat spasming with the effort.

Tiny hands touched the woven-wire fence. "Hi."

Augusta looked away, as if the voice had come from across the street. The last time she'd seen that face was the day she handed over her sleeping baby. She thought she'd felt the worst pain of her life on that day; she didn't know the ache would persist, that it would stab her in the night and torture her days.

A voice called from the house, "Charlotte, come inside, dear. Come along, come along."

I named her Charlotte but called her Lottie. Now she is someone else's Charlotte.

Augusta's sensible shoes headed for the other side of town, where the leaves fell on cracked, uneven sidewalks.

Chapter One

Farm Life

In 1906, twelve-year-old Augusta knew already that life was not easy. There was always work to be done in the house, in the fields, or in the barns. She was strong enough to work with the men, but her mother kept her in or near the house. The closest she got to farmwork was collecting eggs or helping in the vegetable garden. Housework and the feeding of family and farmhands filled her day.

She'd be allowed to attend school long enough to read and write, add and subtract, but when she was old enough to be of use on the farm her education would end. She was entering eighth grade, in school longer than any of her siblings, but the school stopped at eighth grade. She'd have to move to another town to continue her education, but she was needed on the farm.

Her brother Joseph was only a year older, but he'd been pulled from school in fifth grade. He'd liked school, and encouraged his little sister to study and do well. He read her school books when no one was looking. The older boys learned long ago not to speak of dreams or complain, because Papa didn't want to hear it. Their father was kind and gentle when they were younger, but when they were old enough to be of use on the farm he stopped being Papa and became The Boss.

As Joseph got taller his workload increased, and time to talk with Augusta while they shucked corn or pulled carrots became more valuable. "Ya know, Papa only sent us ta school ta get us outta the way when we were too small ta work." Joseph pulled up a carrot, sending a bit of dirt into his eye.

"That's what ya get fer talkin' 'bout Papa like that." Augusta handed him a hanky.

"Why do women carry things like this?" He dabbed at his eye.

"Cuz men do stupid things an' expect us ta fix it."

"Why'd ya embroider flowers on a rag ya blow your nose on?" He handed it back. "Ya din't blow yer nose on that, did ya?"

"No." She folded it back into the pocket she'd sewn onto her feed-sack dress. "The flowers are fer me. They make me feel better. And why'd ya care, so long as it got the mud outta yer eye?"

"Come on, Gus, I know ya dream a better things. Don't cha wish ya could stay in school an' learn enough ta get outta this mud? I din't get ta sixth grade—what could I do 'cept farm?"

"Don't call me Gus."

"You used ta like it when I called ya Gus."

"I'm growed up now." She raised her face to the sun, which had just popped from behind the clouds. "I'd like ta live in a fine house, an' it'd be nice ta wear real dresses ever' day."

Joseph asked, "Why ya wearin' a rope belt? I gave ya my old leather belt, it looks better'n that."

"I save that fer school. Workin' round the farm, my belt don't matter."

Their conversation was cut short when the older boys drove into the barnyard towing their broken tractor with the neighbor's truck. Joseph was happy to step in front of his two older brothers to figure out what was wrong. They couldn't deny he had an eye for machinery.

* * *

Augusta was as excited about getting a new dress as she was about the eighth-grade graduation ceremony. This would be her first store-bought dress. She'd outgrown her hand-me-down and efforts to let it out left clear marks where stitching had been altered.

Augusta wore that hand-me-down when she went to town with Mama to buy her new dress. They walked into Ferguson's General Store, Mama standing tall, Augusta's eyes wide as she saw the shelves of dresses and a pretty pink one displayed on a hanger. She browsed the few choices while Mama shopped for household needs. Mama shook her head when Augusta held up her choice, made of pale green fabric with a faint red thread running through it and gold trim on the collar.

"Graduation dresses have ta be white." She could see her daughter's disappointment. "All the other girls'll be wearin' white. I don't know why graduation dresses are white, but they are."

There were only two white dresses left; other graduates

had already been there. The one Augusta liked was too small, and neither she nor Mama liked the look of the other one. Augusta had resigned herself to having the least attractive white dress in her class when Mama held up a dress that was prettier than any Augusta had seen, and said, "Somebody hid this'n under a pile a dungarees."

That white dress fit perfectly, and the price fell within what Mama could afford. But Mama held up the dress to the store clerk and asked how they could charge such a price for a simple dress. She dickered until the clerk called the owner from the back room. Augusta stared at her feet, embarrassed by the exchange, resigning herself yet again to the ugly dress. But Mama knew what she was doing, and was already on the sidewalk when Augusta walked out the door and heard the clerk behind her say, "I pity the man who's gotta live with that woman."

Mama was smiling, with the perfect white dress wrapped in paper tucked under her arm. "Shopkeepers don't know how hard money is ta come by fer people who don't stand in one place all day."

Augusta was as proud of that dress as she was of her diploma. Her friend Cookie didn't get a new dress, but her mama gussied up a hand-me-down from her older sister's graduation—you couldn't tell it'd been put together from pieces. If Cookie was embarrassed it didn't show as she twirled to show Augie her new dress. If they didn't acknowledge that it wasn't new, it didn't matter.

Both girls had worn sacks of some sort for most of their lives. Flour sacks were softer and prettier than feed sacks. The girls and their mothers looked for sacks with interesting designs or pretty lettering. They were adept at cutting sleeve holes to look like cups, and if there was extra thread they'd create a collar of sorts and sew on pockets cut from their worn-out sack dresses.

Augusta's brothers had all been pulled from school in fifth or sixth grade. Their work was "more valuable than anythin' they could learn in school." Augusta heard those words again when Papa wanted to "stop this foolish schoolin'" before she reached seventh grade. Mama didn't question Papa often, but she did that day. "Augusta's reward fer bein' handy shouldn't stop 'er from gettin' 'er eighth-grade diploma."

When Augusta heard that discussion over dinner she remembered the previous spring, when she and Mama had stayed up all night.

Chapter Two

Bella's Calf

The hip-roof barn behind the house loomed in the twilight, its gray frame, three stories high, seemed even taller looking up at it from the faint glow of the kerosene lantern Mama carried. Bella, their best cow, had been tethered for the past two days where she could be seen from the house. Augusta had seen many births on the farm, but this one caused a fuss she'd never witnessed. When Mama saw wax on Bella's teats, she announced, "We should have us a calf by tomorra."

Augusta led Bella while Mama opened the door to the barn, where they would all spend the night. The barn's rough-sawn plank walls were unpainted on the inside. The six rarely-used box stalls along one wall were solid and strong, but the livestock mostly lived outside. They were brought in if sick or injured, but most deliveries happened unattended out in the fields. Papa taught her to wait until the cow and calf were up and about, then to drag the afterbirth to the pigsty and toss it over the fence. Otherwise, the dogs might get into it and Papa said the dogs' job was keeping coyotes and foxes from going after the stock. He didn't want the dogs thinking there was a meal for them anywhere but in the bowls he fed them from. The dogs ate in one place every morning, and weren't allowed anything else.

The pigs were another story; they'd eat almost anything. Mama said if a person died in the pigpen, they'd be gone in a day or two, bones and all. Papa said the only thing that kept the hogs from eating up the whole damned farm was the heavy wire fencing. They could stick their snouts through but, try as they might, even the biggest sow couldn't bend that wire.

Augusta patted Bella's neck as she closed them all into a twelve-foot-square stall for the night. Bella had been bred to an expensive bull, which made the calf valuable. Mama was worried about how much had been spent, and Papa was hoping the calf would more than pay back the breeding fee.

The barn was warm, the stall clean and well bedded. The other side of the barn was almost empty. Last fall the loft had been full of hay and straw, so the excess had been stacked here in neat rows of green-and-yellow bales. The lower stores were used up before Christmas, and the loft would be nearly empty before the hay and grains on the farm were harvested.

They'd been in the barn for a couple hours when Bella's water broke and she lay down. When there was no progress for almost an hour, Mama said, "I'm afraid this calf might be comin' backwards."

Augusta lifted her tipping head—she couldn't fall asleep, she was there to help. Mama looked her way. "When I was yer age I dreamed 'bout gettin' off the farm. Marryin' a doctor or somethin', an' livin' in town."

Augusta never heard Mama talk like that, and was now

wide awake. Her mother continued, "I lived near a bigger town, so long ago I can't remember its name. There were town-kids in school, an' they had nicer clothes an' could afford new books, not the ole ripped-up kind the farm kids got fer free. I wished I had a new book that was my own. Sometimes three of us had one book 'tween us."

Augusta thought of the two books that sat upright on Mama's bureau. No one was allowed to touch them. *Did she ever read them? When would she have had the time?*

Mama's gaze softened with memory. "I was in a house once that had a room full a books. Ever' wall was a bookcase. Seemed the windows were only there fer light ta read by." Her eyes glistened in the yellow glow from the lantern hanging above.

She patted Bella. "Come on, lady, give us a healthy calf. It'd be nice ta get a bull calf." She patted the cow again. "A bull calf from this bloodline'd bring farmers here ta breed their stock. Bella, m' dear, it'd be no more trouble ta deliver a bull than a cow calf, so let's make it a bull."

Mama leaned against the wall with one hand resting on Bella, the rough-sawn wood catching strands of her graying hair. "My papa thought bull calves were more valuable, an' so were the boys. I was his only daughter an' he was glad of it."

She looked at Augusta. "You'd think that woulda made me a jewel to him, but I knew I was less in his eyes. He left me in school cuz I didn't have much worth on the farm. I was in eleventh grade an' lookin' forward to a high school diploma when my mama died. She took sick, an' in two days she was gone. My papa said, 'It's a good thing she taught ya how ta take care a the house when yer nose wasn't stuck in a book.'

"My mama was still warm in the next room when my papa stood in the kitchen and raised his arms ta declare, 'This house is yers ta take care a now.' Then he cried the longest, loudest weepin' I ever heard from a growed man."

Her hand jumped from Bella's side, the cow gave a soft moan, and a white bubble appeared under her tail. Within that bubble was a hoof, and a second hoof appeared as Bella began to push her calf into the world. Mama smiled. "This calf is right side up an' on its way."

The calf's nose appeared next, lying flat against its front legs. Augusta had watched many calves and foals dive from their mamas—like someone diving off a rock and entering the water fingers-first, arms straight, head and upper arms together. She was shocked to learn that human babies came into the world headfirst. She thought diving made more sense.

Mama grabbed the calf's ankles and said, "Come over here an' I'll show ya how ta do this. Bella's not havin' trouble, but if a calf is comin' hard, this is how ya can lend a hand."

Augusta took an ankle in each hand and followed her mother's directions. She had to get a firm grip because the little ankles slid around under the sack that contained this new life. "Now, when ya feel Bella push, pull down, slow an' steady. Pull the calf toward Bella like the calf is a crescent moon."

The hind feet were barely out when Mama cleared the placenta away from the calf's face and ran her fingers around in its mouth, waiting for that first breath.

Augusta had seen a stillborn foal once. One of their workhorse mares had a foal that never pushed itself out of the sack; it just lay there, not moving. She ran and got Papa, but when he arrived he stood there for a few minutes and said, "Stillborn. This sometimes happens."

He patted Augusta's head. "You stay here an' watch till Elma stops tryin' ta make 'er baby get up. When she walks away, ya go get one a yer brothers an' have him throw the foal in with the hogs." He looked at Elma before walking away. "Sorry, girl."

Augusta watched Elma nuzzle the foal, making little noises she'd never heard from a horse—not a whinny or a neigh, but a whisper. She pawed gently with her huge hooves, trying to wake her baby. She took the foal's ear in her teeth and lifted its head, then let it drop, then started all over again. Augusta wanted to leave rather than watch the sad scene, but she'd been told to watch. It seemed like hours before Elma gave up and walked away, and Augusta ran off to get Joseph.

He followed her to the field pushing a wheelbarrow, picked up the foal, set it inside, and wheeled it toward the pigsty. Augusta asked, "Why'd we have ta wait so long to take the foal away?"

Joseph didn't turn his head; he didn't want to spill the foal. "Papa says if ya take the baby away fore the mama gives up on it, she'll call and call fer days, lookin' fer 'er baby. If you wait till she knows it's gone, she'll go on without all that fuss."

Now, Bella's healthy calf lay on its side in the straw with the cord still attached while Augusta and Mama rubbed its damp body with handfuls of straw. Bella looked around at them like she approved. Mama said, "We should wait till the cord stops pulsin' fore we break it."

This was news to Augusta. Out in the field, the cord breaks when the calf or the cow stands up. When the cord stopped pulsing, Augusta watched her mother hold it in her fist, near the calf's belly, and pull it apart with her other hand. Then Mama took a clean cloth, poured whiskey on it, and applied it to the stub, smiling at Augusta. "Rich people use medicine ta disinfect, we use hooch."

She lifted up the calf's tail. "One hole, we got us a bull calf." Then Mama laughed long and hard.

Augusta understood her mama was relieved to have a healthy bull calf on the ground, but she didn't understand why she was laughing like that. Augusta was wondering if her mama had lost her mind, when she finally stopped laughing and settled back in the straw, staring up at the ceiling. That was worse.

"Mama, are ya all right?"

"I ain't never been so all right."

* * *

The sky was silver in the east beyond the mountain ridgeline when Augusta and her mother walked back to the house to wash up and start breakfast. When Papa walked into the kitchen Mama didn't look up from her work. "It's a bull calf an' he's up an' nursin'."

Papa took the spatula from Mama's hand, turned her

around, and lifted her from the floor, twirling her around, knocking over chairs in the process. They were both laughing. When he saw his daughter slack-jawed in the corner, he set Mama down, handed her the spatula, and said, "Maybe I should go out an' check on things."

As he turned away, Mama slapped him on his backside and said, "Ya just do that."

Augusta had never seen her parents share affection. She and Joseph had wondered how they'd produced so many children when they didn't seem to even like each other. She couldn't wait to tell him what she'd just seen.

After breakfast Augusta was sent to gather the raspberries that grew along the roadside fence. When a neighbor boy stopped to talk about nothing in particular, Mama came out on the porch with a broom in hand, shouting, "Herbert Samson, ya just let 'er be. She's got work ta do and so do ya. Get on outta here or ya'll feel this broom handle."

He stood there a moment longer, just to show that he could, and told Augusta, "That woman's mean as a snake."

When Herbert was out of earshot, Augusta said to herself, "No, she's just tired."

Chapter Three

Cookie

Cookie was out of school three days in a row. It was the last week of classes, with eighth-grade graduation in the offing. *Where is she?* Augusta planned to march over to her house after school to find out, but when she got home, Mama had news, and it wasn't good.

"Betty Church is deathly sick. I want ya ta take these biscuits an' stew over ta their house an' see if they have any chores ya can help with."

Augusta accepted the basket and said, "I was wonderin' why Cookie wasn't in school."

"Now don't be callin''er Cookie in front a Mrs. Church. Ya know 'er name's Clara. 'Er mama don't like that nickname, so don't be causin' trouble at a time like this." She placed a towel over the basket of warm food.

"I'll be good." Augusta adjusted her grip on the basket that was heavy with food for the whole Church family. Cookie had three older brothers who ate like farmhands, because they were. Her older sister, Marion, had run off last spring with a coal miner from up north, so that left one less mouth to feed but two less hands to help. The screen door was closing behind Augusta when her mama said, "Tell Mr. Church I 'spect ya home fore dark."

"Yes, Mama." She'd be quicker walking home, with an empty basket.

Augusta mused as she switched the basket from hand to hand. *Why does Mrs. Church hate the name Cookie?* Then she wondered why her mama didn't like it when her brothers called her Gus. Cookie called her Augie, but not in front of Mama, after she once made that mistake. "Her name is Augusta, not Augie or Gus or Gussie, an' ya just keep that in mind, Clara Church."

Augusta and Clara had been friends since the first day of school. It was like they'd known one another before they'd ever met. By appearance, they were nearly opposite. Clara was tiny, with blond hair and deep-blue eyes. Her hands were so small, they fluttered around her voice like butterflies when she was excited. No one called Augusta tiny. She was of average height, but solid. Not overweight, but sturdy. Her hair was somewhere between black and brown, a combination of her mother's raven locks and her father's sandy brown. Her eyes were a blend of her parent's contradictions: her mother's deep pools of dark brown and her father's hazel that changed color like a chameleon. Augusta's eyes were brown, plain and simple, like everything else about her.

Augie and Cookie's nicknames were one secret among many the girls shared. Augusta was sad they might not graduate eighth grade together, but pushed that out of her head. If her mama was sick, Cookie needed to be there.

Augusta expected the house to be quiet and sad, but heard laughter as she stepped onto the porch. Cookie opened the door and announced, "Augie, Mama's made a turn, she's feelin' so much better. It's like a miracle or somethin'." She whispered the last words, because Mr. Church was not a religious man and didn't believe in nonsense like miracles. He would have thought his last name a joke on God, if he believed in God. Mrs. Church hadn't been inside a church since she got married, but she taught her children to believe and pray. The boys didn't take to it, but Cookie was her mother's daughter.

Augusta set the basket on the kitchen table and announced, "Mama sent beef stew an' biscuits."

Mrs. Church looked pale and tired, but she always looked tired. Augusta had been told that tired was a woman's lot in life.

Mrs. Church took the food from the basket and set it in the warming bin on the side of the woodstove. "I'll keep this warm till the boys come in. Thank yer mama fer me, and tell 'er I'll return the stew pot tomorra."

"It's okay, she's got another." Augusta was looking around to see what work she might be needed for.

"Good neighbors don't keep what ain't theirs any longer than they got ta. Clara or one a the boys'll get this pot back tomorra. Augusta Young, what're ya lookin' fer?"

"Mama said I should help out, but I don't see much needs doin'."

"Your mama's gift took care a the only chore ain't done, an' I thank her. Now I can sit a spell fore dinner."

Cookie pulled out a chair. "Yeah, Mama, sit down. I'll set the table an' all fore the boys come in."

"Clara, you're the light a my life." They looked at one another in a way Augusta and her mother never did.

"Well, if ya don't have work fer me, I'll get on home."

Augusta was walking toward the door.

Cookie jumped up. "I'll walk part way with ya." She looked back at Mrs. Church, who'd already gotten up to load wood in the stove. "I'll take care a the fire in a minute, Mama, you just sit."

The girls were barely off the porch when Cookie whispered, "Mama was so sick we thought we were gonna lose her. Then this mornin' she got outta bed, made breakfast, and went about like any other day. I stayed home cuz I was afraid it wouldn't last. Sometimes the influenza rests a bit fore it hits its hardest."

Augusta said, "My mama said she's at death's door."

"She was, yesterday." With that Cookie turned, calling over her shoulder, "I don't wanna leave her alone too long. If things look good tomorra, I'll see ya in school."

Augusta watched her friend walk away. "I'll meet ya at the creek."

* * *

The next morning, Augusta approached the bend in the creek, worried Cookie wouldn't be there. The mountains around her were in a haze of fog, their purple shadows like a bad omen, but Cookie sat on a rock, waiting with a smile. They exchanged nods and Cookie pointed to a hollow log. "I put your mama's stew pot in there. Don't forget to fetch it on yer way home. It was good to have your mama's help for dinner last night, but my mama'll be mad if that pot ain't returned today."

They proceeded down the dusty road toward the makeshift school. They didn't have a real schoolhouse with a bell on top to call students in. Theirs was an abandoned log cabin, put into use when someone decided school was important for children. Before then, parents who knew how to read and write taught their children, but most adults in that part of Arkansas hadn't been to school at all.

Cookie announced, "Mama got up this mornin' an' had coffee an' breakfast goin' fore the sun come up. She seemed normal, 'cept fer a cough once in a while."

A dozen students milled around the dry, packed soil in front of the schoolhouse. Some sat on rocks or leaned against trees, but Augusta and Cookie marched in the door to claim chairs before they were all taken. The schoolhouse had no desks, and the few donated chairs were rickety. There was a table the teacher used as a desk, but students worked from their laps or lay on their bellies to use the floorboards as a desk. They used broken pieces of chalkboard for their lessons. Augusta and Clara took two chairs and set them next to one another.

Their teacher, Miss Carpenter, sat at her table. She always seemed busy when they walked in the door. Miss Carpenter was only a few years older than Augusta, and had gone to school in the same room she taught in. Mr. Church didn't think much of Abigail Carpenter, and said, "She don't know no more'n the young'ns she's teachin'. They should be givin' her lessons." Simon Church had strong opinions about everything and everyone.

The girls liked their teacher and enjoyed going to school. Most students didn't make it past sixth grade. The eighth-grade class consisted of four girls and one boy, named Paul, who was crippled from polio. He had a reserved seat with a board leaned against it, so he had something of a desk to work from.

Miss Carpenter glanced at her grandfather's pocket watch, worn like a necklace, at just the right time each morning, and walked out on the porch with an old buggy wrench in her hand. A metal triangle hung on a hook near the door, and when she clanged it with the wrench, children dawdling outside came in and the school day began.

Chapter Four

Graduation

Augusta's dress was perfectly pressed the morning of her graduation. She'd tried it on so many times, she had to use the iron, warmed over the woodstove, to get rid of the wrinkles she'd created. As she put it on, she was surprised by the butterflies fluttering in her stomach. She twirled, remembering the night she and Mama delivered Bella's calf. *Mama didn't get the graduation she'd hoped for, but mine is today.*

The ceremony took place at the town hall. The schoolhouse was too small and dingy for a celebration with as many as thirty people in attendance. The five graduates, with their parents and siblings, walked into the hall on Saturday morning, conversation and laughter echoing off the high ceiling.

The minister began with a blessing, and Augusta's mind wandered. She could see Cookie on the other side of the aisle. Her friend looked so grown-up that, for the first time, the name Clara suited her. Miss Carpenter took her place at the front of the room to give her speech, but Augusta's attention was distracted by the beautiful dress her teacher wore. It was a lovely shade of green with white collar and cuffs and a dark-green bow at her throat, with a matching bow in her hair. The dress reminded Augusta of the first dress she'd picked out at Ferguson's. Miss Carpenter began calling out names of graduates to come up and receive their diplomas, and Augusta's attention returned. Paul and his family sat in the front row, and his name was called first. Paul's father helped him walk the few feet to the podium, and when they sat down Augusta was called.

Her legs wobbled as she stood. Seconds ago they'd been solid, but her knees had turned to water. She managed to get to the podium and accept the paper that was handed to her, but when Miss Carpenter congratulated her, she felt her lips move but no words came out. She managed to return a smile before wobbling back to her chair.

Seated next to her mother, Augusta pored over the most impressive piece of paper she'd ever seen, and it was hers. It was certified by the State of Arkansas, her name was there in official black print, and at the bottom was the signature of some very important person. Her mother patted her back and Augusta held her diploma out to her. Her mother's fingers slid along the embossed seal next to the important signature.

The group gathered in a smaller meeting room after the ceremony for tea, milk, and cookies. They milled around, parents talking to parents, children fussing and fidgeting. Augusta saw Cookie and Mr. Church, and before she could wonder where Mrs. Church was she heard a cough, reminding her that a muffled cough had been in the background during the ceremony. Mrs. Church sat off to the side and her family hovered around her. She was ill.

* * *

Augusta walked through the back door with her diploma. She wasn't gawking over it now, but she did place it in the cigar box of treasures under her bed. It lay atop a sparkling pin Mama had given her, strands of ribbons of various colors, a couple of crayons, a handful of marbles, hairpins, a comb, and a photograph of someone she didn't know. She'd found it in the trash at Ferguson's General Store and saved it, because photos were rare and valuable.

Her graduation dress hung on a peg as she pulled her flour-sack dress over her head, employing a piece of rope for a belt. They'd been planning a family celebration of roast chicken with all the fixings and apple pie for dessert, Augusta's favorite, but that changed when Betty Church took sick. Mama prepared the planned meal, but wrapped it up and walked it over to the Church family.

Augusta watched the chicken simmer on the stove, its bubbling reminding her of the cough she'd ignored at the town hall. Papa and Mama took her favorite meal to the Church family and volunteered their family's assistance as long as Betty was ill. Augusta and her family ate soup and stale bread for supper.

* * *

Augusta had a diploma, the first of her siblings with that distinction. She often looked through her cache in the cigar box before going to sleep at night. She shared her room with her sister Helen. If Helen was sleeping, Augusta would reach down in the dark to fumble the lid open and touch her riches. She knew what they looked like.

Her diploma was only a few days old when it disappeared. She reached into the darkness and ran her fingers over her pin, but the paper it had been resting on was gone. Her fingers groped among hairpins, marbles, a couple of pennies, and bits of ribbon, but she knew what had happened. Joseph had been jealous of what he called her "fancy graduation paper." She knew how much he'd wanted to stay in school, how much he wanted a diploma. She was sure he'd taken it and probably burned it in the kitchen stove. But she didn't understand why.

Augusta loved to talk with Joseph when no one else was around, because he'd say things Papa wouldn't have liked. If they complained, Papa would lecture about hard work. If they were especially happy, they got the same lecture. Hard work was his answer to everything. Augusta and Joseph shared secrets about simple things, like sadness, joy, or disappointment. Joseph had encouraged her to work hard in school, and now she was sure he'd taken her diploma.

Thievery among the children was not tolerated. If one of them took something that wasn't theirs, they were punished. Papa's belt was thick and strong, and everyone had felt it at one time or another, especially the older boys. Augusta would announce her loss in the morning, and Joseph would get the belt.

Mama and the girls had been up for over an hour when the boys stumbled in for breakfast. The kitchen smelled of coffee and bacon and bustled with idle conversation and the sound of chairs scraping the worn wooden floor. The table consisted of long planks resting on sawhorses, which made it easy to move into the yard during Arkansas's hot summer days. That morning it was laden with bacon, scrambled eggs, and biscuits fresh and steaming. Each person had their designated seat, with the youngest sitting at the sawhorses, where they had to maneuver their legs awkwardly. You got the seat you were dealt and you lived with it.

Augusta straddled a sawhorse leg as she sat down next to Joseph. They didn't speak. They didn't look at one another. There was plenty of conversation in the room, so no one noticed the gulf between them. They ate their food in silence.

Mama noticed that Joseph was eating slower than usual and asked, "Are ya feelin' all right, Joseph?" The two older boys were wiping up the last bits of bacon grease with their biscuits, and Joseph was not half done. Mama looked at Augusta's plate. "Are you two tryin' ta be last so ya can jabber over the cleanup?"

Augusta set her fork down. "I'm just not very hungry."

"You'll eat what's in front a ya. We don't waste food 'round here." Papa had rules.

The older boys volunteered at the same time: "I'll eat it."

Augusta held up her plate and it was grabbed out of her hand. Papa's chair screeched back and he looked at Mama. "Talk ta her." He stood up. "Joseph, I 'spect ya in the barn in five minutes." He looked at his pocket watch, tucked it back into his bib-overall pocket, and walked off.

Augusta hadn't said anything about the diploma. She didn't actually want to get Joseph in trouble. She went about cleaning up after the meal, rehearsing what she wanted to say to him later, when nobody was around.

Chapter Five

Betty Church

In the weeks that followed, Augusta spent every spare moment helping Cookie feed and care for the Church household. Performing the chores Betty Church had tended to for most of her life required the efforts of two hardworking girls.

Clara cared for her sick mother, trying to get Betty to take her medicine, drink broth, or eat a little bread. They watched as Mrs. Church became frail. Wrists that had been strong enough to carry a bale of hay in each hand looked like they would snap lifting a teacup. Her eyes looked out from between ridges of cheekbone and brow. Clara tried to keep her hair clean and brushed, but it soon became too much for Betty's neck to support her own head.

"Augie, can you help me in here?" Clara was bent over her mother's slight frame.

Augusta stood in the doorway. Each time she saw Mrs. Church, she was surprised by how thin and gray she looked. Clara had a bottle in her left hand, a spoon in her right. "I need 'er ta take this medicine, but I'm afraid if she isn't sitting up enough she'll choke. Can ya sit 'er up a little?"

"Why don't I spoon the medicine while you hold 'er?" Augusta was afraid Mrs. Church would break if she tried to move her.

Clara handed off the medicine and carefully lifted her mother to near-sitting. She cradled her mother's chin in her left hand while holding her up with her right arm. "Okay, Augie, we just need ta get one good spoonful down."

Augusta filled the spoon and got it to Betty's lips, but they didn't move. Clara deftly opened her mother's mouth enough to fit the spoon into it. Augusta tipped the spoon, and Clara closed her mother's mouth. Mrs. Church didn't swallow.

"Come on, Mama, ya have ta take this medicine." She stroked her mother's throat, like she was petting a kitten, until she swallowed.

Augusta was glad to work on cooking and keeping the house clean. She collected eggs from the henhouse, made sure the layers had food and water, and kept the coop up. She remembered how her mama made her dumplings, but couldn't get the gravy right. Mr. Church and his sons never complained, and sometimes even complimented her cooking efforts. The boys ate supper, then disappeared back to the barn or up to their rooms. Mr. Church seemed lost after supper. He looked in on his wife, but not for long. Then he sat on the porch and gazed at the mountains in the distance.

Augusta felt guilty about the relief she felt when she went home at night. It was nice to hear people speaking in normal tones. She was sitting on the porch steps watching the fireflies when Joseph sat down next to her. "How's it goin' over there?"

"She's dyin' an' Clara won't admit it. It's hard ta watch."

"It's good yer there ta help out."

"Sometimes I don't feel like I'm doin' much good. There's just nothin' that helps."

"Yer doin' good, Gus. Yer a good friend." They sat in silence until the fireflies flickered out, then went to bed.

Helen was asleep, and Augusta reached into the darkness under her bed to survey her cigar-box treasures. She touched the pin her mother had given her, thought about how she would feel if her mother were dying, and shuddered. She felt a piece of paper under the pin and knew it was her diploma. *How long has it been there?* She hadn't checked on her treasures for days. She reviewed her blessings as she fell asleep; the list was long.

* * *

Augusta and Clara spoke in quiet tones while they gave Mrs. Church a sponge bath. Betty wasn't talking anymore, but they never called one another by their nicknames in front of her. When Mrs. Church was clean and dressed in a fresh nightgown, Clara washed whatever laundry needed doing. Augusta looked down at Betty and asked Clara, "Do ya think we should leave her alone?"

Clara smiled and brushed her mama's forehead. "She's doin' much better today." Augusta shook her head as they left the room.

The galvanized washtub stood on two chairs on the back porch. The girls hauled water from the hand pump that jutted from the ground between the house and the barn, and heated it over the woodstove. There was a washboard on either side of the tub and, standing opposite one another, the girls soaked the clothes in the warm water and applied soap from a naphtha bar. The yellow-brown soap produced enough lather to wash away most dirt and grime. They'd rub the cloth between their hands and revert to the rippled washboard for dirtier items. When the fabric seemed clean, they'd wring it out over the tub and rinse it in a bucket of clean water at their feet before hanging it on the clothesline to dry.

They could talk in normal voices out there. Clara scrubbed at the manure-stained cuffs on her father's trousers, saying, "Mama's lookin' better, don't ya think?"

Augusta searched for something positive to say. "She drank more soup." She was sure that wasn't true, but couldn't think of anything that might indicate Mrs. Church would recover. She'd stopped talking days ago and looked like a skeleton with gray-brown skin hung over it. Her hair had turned white. Augusta wished Clara would stop trying to make her mother's hair look better, because it became thinner with each brushing. Her ears stood out through what was left of it, and she looked like an abandoned doll.

Clara wiped soap from her cheek. "Yeah, I think she likes the chicken soup better'n the vegetable. I'll ask one a the boys ta slaughter a chicken tomorra."

Augusta didn't think chicken would make any difference, but it couldn't hurt, and the boys would enjoy having meat for dinner. Roasting a chicken was one of the recipes she had confidence in, and maybe the gravy would come out better this time. Augusta said, "I'll simmer the carcass to a healthy broth. I wish we could leave some meat in it for 'er."

Clara began to cry. "Mama can't remember how to chew."

The clothes lay in the wash water while the girls held one another. They'd never hugged before. "Augie, she's gonna die, ain't she?"

Hearing her nickname whispered in her ear gave Augusta the strength to say what she'd been thinking. "Cookie, I don't know how she's lasted this long."

They cried in one another's arms until they heard the barn door sliding on its track. They stepped apart and went back to work.

Mr. Church walked up the porch steps and passed the girls without a word. They looked at one another with questions in their eyes. Simon Church never came back into the house after he'd started his workday. They rarely saw him before supper. Augusta asked Clara, "Is he sick?"

She answered, "He don't look it."

They were both back to the washing when he walked out the door and said, "She's gone."

Both girls dropped their work. Simon's eyes never left the horizon as he said, "You two finish what yer doin'. Then, Augusta, you go get yer mama an' she'll help us get ready fer a wake."

The girls didn't move. Augusta listened to birds chirping as if nothing were wrong, until Simon bellowed, "Now get ta work, ya got things ta do."

He walked toward the barn, but when he got to the pump he dropped to all fours, like he was looking for something lost in the dirt, then he hugged that old pump like a long-lost friend, his body shaking with grief.

Augusta could hardly remember what followed. They finished the laundry, probably not very well, and she ran home to tell her mama what had happened. Her brother

Joseph was sent to town to tell the minister and set the
neighbors to the tasks they would take on.

Chapter Six

Gone to Grave

Augusta and her mother walked to the Church home wearing real dresses. Augusta wore her tattered hand-me-down, as her graduation dress seemed inappropriate. Mama carried a basket with sachets and herbs.

When they walked into the house all was quiet; the clock on the mantel had been stopped and the door to the room where Betty lay was open. Clara sat next to her mother's body, wearing her graduation dress. Her tears had stopped, but their evidence clung to her face. She said, "I ironed Mama's dress." It hung on the wall with sprigs of lavender pinned to its bodice. The mirror on the wall beside it was draped in black.

Clara, Augusta, and her mama went to work carefully washing Betty Church and putting her in her only dress. They paused in their work when a bell in the distance peeled three times. Cookie's brothers brought in a wooden cot of sorts, and the women placed blankets and pillows on it to make Betty more comfortable. When the three of them moved what was left of her body onto that bier, she weighed less than the blanket she lay on.

They carried her delicate body on its stiff wooden cot into the main room of the house and began the wake. Someone had to sit with the body day and night until she could be buried. They each took a chair, but no words were exchanged until Augie said to Cookie, "She's in a better place."

Augusta struggled for something more to say when her mama said to Cookie, "Yer mama was a fine woman. Ya should be proud ta be 'er daughter."

They spoke in muted tones, aware that the pounding in the barn was Betty's coffin being built.

Paul's mother, Ida, and Abigail Carpenter were the first to arrive. They carried baskets of cleaning tools and nodded sad hellos as they walked through the room. Abigail rested a hand on Clara's shoulder as she passed and said, "Yer mama's in a better place."

Augusta wondered how many times she would hear those words in the coming hours.

In the bedroom, Helen and Abigail went to work, stripping the bed and setting the bedding aside to be washed. The window curtains came down and Helen carried them with the bedding to the back porch, where the washtub stood. They went about cleaning every corner of the room, every surface wiped clean. The floor, walls, and ceiling were washed.

Augusta heard women on the back porch, preparing to wash the bedding and curtains, their subdued conversation barely audible. They clunked around in the kitchen, warming water for their task. The house was soon full of women and their daughters, cleaning every corner and preparing food for themselves and the men who gathered in the barn.

Some in the barn were overseeing the construction of a coffin, others brought cows in from the field, fed and milked them, fed other livestock, and set the barn straight. Clara's brothers were carrying the casket they'd crafted toward the house when Betty's brother James arrived. He motioned for them to stop and set it down. His lanky body knelt beside the box, and he reached under his best jacket to pull out a tiny pink pillow, which he set inside the coffin. He returned to standing, like a marionette being pulled by its blond hair, and the boys carried the coffin to the house.

When they set the casket on the floor, Clara, Augusta, and her mama lifted Betty using the blanket she lay on, and set her softly inside. Mama pulled the pink pillow from under the blanket and lifted Betty's head to let it rest on her brother's gift. They stood back and Clara's brothers set the coffin on the bier and went back outside. The women folded the blanket around Betty and sprinkled it with fragrant herbs. Betty looked like she'd just laid down for a nap.

Mama said, "Carol's making 'er fried chicken."

Clara looked down at her mother's gaunt face. "It ain't near as good as yers, Mama. No one can make fried chicken as good as yers." Tears eased down her cheeks.

The smell of ammonia and soap was overwhelmed by the fragrances of ham and chicken mingling with coffee and biscuits. The men lingered outside until they got word all was ready within.

* * *

Betty Church was laid to rest on a sunny afternoon. The day after she died, her house was full of flowers. The women and daughters of her community had gathered every flower they could find from gardens, pastures, wood lots, and roadsides. The abundance of floral arrangements was testimony to their regard. Someone created a harp of flowers, the strings carefully placed except for the center one, which hung broken.

The Church family couldn't afford a stone marker, but Betty's brother James borrowed a grave marker kit from the town mortician. The bag of cement he bought was an extravagance he couldn't afford, but Betty was his only sister and they'd been close.

James asked Joseph to help him because Joseph had a talent for such things. They poured wet cement into a rectangular mold and used the metal letters and numbers to press into the drying cement the words Betty had wanted. Simon stayed away because he knew they'd put some religious nonsense on there. Betty Louise Church had a real marker with the poem she'd asked James for.

> Just have an old-fashioned preacher
> To preach a sermon or two
> Don't spend your money on flowers
> Just a rose will do

Joseph had a talent for carving doves and flowers into wood and getting the words straight and level, so he'd carved many wooden grave markers. But he'd never pressed metal letters into cement. When it was done the words looked straight and even, but he thought it needed more. James thought the letters were perfect. Joseph fetched Augusta. "Look at this. What d'ya think?"

"It looks handsome, but ya don't look happy with it."

Joseph replied, "I'm used ta carvin', I know how ta do that. This cement is different. I'd like ta put some flowers in it, but I dunno if it'll work, and I don't have enough cement left to fix it if I mess up. It looks so plain."

"Can't ya scratch a rose into the cement?"

"What if I mess it up?"

"What if ya don't?"

Joseph soon discovered he was as good at scratching images into cement as he was at carving them into wood.

Augusta thought the roses looked soft, twining around the poem. "I like it."

* * *

The funeral was held in the home Betty Church had raised her children in. Simon didn't like it, but he knew his wife wanted a minister present. When the praying part of things began, Simon stood in the doorway, as far away as he could get without leaving altogether. His sons and their cousins carried the coffin out that door, and he and Clara and the rest of the mourners followed them to the family grave site at the top of the hill beside the house. The distant mountains looked down on this funeral as they had for so many in the past, at the wooden headstones surrounded by a well-kept fence, and Betty's cement marker standing out among them. The coffin's cover was removed and mourners filed by one last time, then Simon set the cover in place and nailed it down, his face as gray and hard as the headstone. Before stepping back, he touched the single rose Joseph had carved into the wooden cover.

Simon's face didn't change as Betty was lowered into the ground, and everyone waited as the young men present filled the hole; it was bad luck to leave before the final prayer was said over the finished soil mound.

With the funeral done, the women went back to work, feeding everyone present in a picnic-like setting on the ground between the house and barn. Families sat on blankets and people mingled, but no games were played. There were jugs of corn liquor in the barn, but they were swigged there, and there they stayed. Betty had told Simon that was her wish and he stuck to it.

The sun set behind the Ozarks all around them, and no one left until the day turned to night.

Chapter Seven

Arrangements Were Made

Augusta's parents encouraged her to continue helping Cookie a few days a week. Mama said, "There's a lot ta do fer one young girl."

Simon liked Augusta's cooking and even complimented her gravy, which was getting better with practice. Augusta came in the afternoon when her work at home was done, and stayed through supper. She could see how tired Cookie was.

One night when Augusta started toward home, Simon said, "I'll be walkin' ya home tonight."

She was surprised by the offer and answered, "That's okay, it ain't nearly dark out."

He took the bag from her hand and said, "I'll carry this fer ya. We got some talkin' ta do."

They walked in silence until they got to the creek, where Simon cleared his throat and started in. "Yer papa an' me been talkin'. Ya been handy 'round the house an' I'm not used ta bein' alone so much."

The back of Augusta's neck went cold. What was he talking about?

"Ya know 'bout men an' women, an' I'm a man. Yer just barely a woman but yer one fer sure."

Her neck turned hot and her stomach churned. They walked in silence until he asked, "Ya got nothin' ta say?"

The silence followed them to her door, where she hoped to escape to her room, but Simon walked into the kitchen behind her.

Her parents sat at the table like they were waiting for her, and they weren't surprised to see Simon. Simon gave her father a questioning look and her mama stood up and said, "Come along, girl."

They went out the door and walked to the bench near the vegetable garden. Mama sat and patted the seat beside her. Augusta didn't want to sit, but when Mama patted the bench again she did, her spine so straight it almost hurt. Mama began, "Did Simon ask ya ta marry him?"

"If that's what he meant, it ain't what he said."

Mama took a breath. "Some men have trouble sayin' things like this. It don't mean he don't mean it. Did you answer?"

"I didn't know he asked."

"Don't be silly, girl. Simon is a good man, he works hard, he's honest, an' he wants you as his wife."

"But, Mama . . ."

"Don't *but, Mama* me. A man like Sim—"

"But Mama, he's so old. He's older than Papa. He's—"

Mama wouldn't let her finish. "He's fit an' strong, an' if you outlive him you'll have children ta take care a ya, an' in the meantime you'll have a home an' a family. Yer papa an' I can't be feedin' ya ferever."

"But, Mama, he don't go to church an' he never let

Cookie or her mama go, neither."

After another deep breath, Mama said, "Betty an' I were longtime friends. That's the only problem she ever had with Simon. She said he was a good husband an' father, an' he earned the respect a churchgoers 'round here by bein' a better man than most a them. She told me she never regretted marryin' Simon.

"No more buts from ya, girl, or ya could just *but* yourself into dyin' alone."

"Mama, I don't love him."

Mama took another long breath. "Love ain't all it's cracked up ta be. A home an' food an' family're more important."

"Ya think I should do this?" Augusta couldn't believe what she was hearing.

"Look at yer choices. No young'ns gonna have a house an' farm ta offer. They won't have a life a hard work ta show ya what they can do. Ya'll be pickin' a pig in a poke an' lucky if ya find anythin' close ta what yer bein' offered."

"Mama, I'm thirteen."

"My mama was twelve when she got married."

"But ya said Cookie's sister was too young ta be runnin' off ta marry, an' she was fifteen."

Mama straightened up for another breath. "It was the runnin' off that was 'er trouble. She knew 'er papa wouldn't approve a that boy. Yer papa approves, I approve, an' ya need ta think 'bout what yer choices are. A good, honest, hardworkin' man ain't easy to come by."

They sat in silence, each waiting for the other to concede. Mama spoke into the darkness. "Ya think about this, really think about yer life, how ya think ya could do better. We'll talk again in the mornin'. I'll go tell the men they'll have their answer tomorra. Yer papa won't be near as easy on ya as I been."

She walked away, leaving Augusta alone in the dark.

Chapter Eight

The Wedding

The days that followed whirled past Augusta like autumn leaves in a windstorm, but the nights were a slow torture. Her mama had told her to think about her life, and that's all she could do when sleep wouldn't come.

That first night, she worried the impending wedding might ruin her friendship with Cookie. An owl called from the tree outside her window and she wished she could fly away into the night. The day after the decision had been made, Augusta arrived at the Church farm as planned, and Cookie greeted her with tea and muffins. She was treated like a guest in the kitchen she'd been working in for weeks.

"Augie, sit down a spell. We got time, I got tons done this mornin'."

Augusta sat, wondering what was happening. Cookie poured tea and served up the muffins Augusta had made two days before. Cookie was all smiles as she announced, "Ya can call me Cookie anytime ya want, now. Papa don't care. He don't care if I call ya Augie, neither. Ya and I can go ta church whenever we want. Papa never let my mama do that. Ya ain't gonna make me call ya Mama, are ya?"

Cookie's laughter set Augusta at ease, and she picked up a muffin. "I thought ya might be mad or somethin'."

"My mama told me she thought Papa would remarry quick. She said, 'He won't be no good by hisself. I told 'er I could take care a the house an' she said, 'That ain't what I'm talkin' 'bout, girl.'"

Cookie giggled. Augusta blushed and asked, "What other deals were made?"

Cookie grabbed the front of the chair seat between her knees and leaned forward. "Well—my papa's gotta treat you right or answer ta yer papa." She giggled again. "Then, yer brother Joseph said ya were a church-goin' Christian, an' he thought ya should be able to go to church."

"Joseph was there?"

"My papa said Joseph sounded like *he* was yer papa half the time."

Augusta hadn't spoken to Joseph yet, she was too embarrassed.

Cookie wriggled in her seat. "Yer mama insisted on a church weddin'. I never thought Papa would agree ta such a thing, but there ya are."

The girls had many such conversations in the days that followed. Simon walked Augusta home every night. He had her sit next to him at the table and occasionally touched her hand a little too long when she passed him a plate or biscuits. "Augusta, ya make the best damned apple pie in the Ozarks."

Augusta had never heard such praise of her cooking, and Simon laughed when she blushed at the compliment. He brushed a wisp of hair off her forehead and she felt a tug that her young body hadn't known. Two nights later he kissed her goodnight at her door, and she felt his lips on hers as she fell asleep that night.

Their wedding was simple but Christian, and Simon stood there like he liked it. There was a party on the grass between their house and the barn, and the whole town showed up with baskets of food and good wishes. Augusta called it *their house* in her mind, and it sounded right.

When night fell the guests went home and Augusta noticed a mule tied to the back of her parent's buckboard. She'd ask Cookie about it when she came back to the house next week—on second thought, she could ask her husband right now.

"Did ya trade a mule fer me?" He was silent too long. "That better be yer best mule."

* * *

She became Augusta Church at the age of thirteen, and Simon's farm was doing better than it ever had. Two years earlier, before Betty got sick, Simon had signed an agreement with the Fordyce Lumber Company. They'd removed every salable tree on his property, paid for the lumber, and provided him with cotton seed. He'd sold most of his livestock, put the pastures into cotton production, and used the money from the lumber to buy a tractor and harvester. The cotton was at full production the year of Augusta's wedding.

Augusta remembered when the trees had disappeared from almost every farm in the area. The lumber company left barren fields where trees once offered shade to pastured livestock. But the farmers had money to buy tractors, and Fordyce provided seed for cotton and strawberries, and apple tree seedlings. Farming near mountains was hard work, and the farmers had been thrilled with the windfall of cash and new opportunities that logging offered, but Augusta missed the trees that had grown in the valleys. She often walked up into the foothills to stand in the remaining forest.

"We got twelve cents a bale," Simon said as he set a package on the table in front of Augusta and another in front of Cookie. They dropped their canning project and tore at the paper. The new store-bought dresses were an unexpected extravagance.

"Come on, now, try 'em on. I wanna see what my girls are gonna look like at the fall doin's."

Augusta sometimes pinched herself to make sure she wasn't dreaming, things were going so well. Simon was kind in ways she'd never expected. Being a wife was a job she'd been training for most of her life, and she was good at it. She was feeling strong and loved.

* * *

"I'm gonna have a baby." They'd just finished dinner and Augusta was clearing the table.

Simon had been walking toward the door, and he spun around. "Are ya sure?"

"We been married fer two years, don't ya think it's 'bout time?"

"Ya thought ya were pregnant last year, and then ya weren't."

"This time I waited till I was sure."

He picked her up and swung her around.

The next day he came back from town with a package for her. She pulled open the paper wrapping and discovered a new dress with a button-flap front to accommodate a growing stomach. "How much did this cost?"

"That's no way ta greet a gift."

"It looks expensive."

"The cotton crop's lookin' good, nearly ready to pick. It's gonna be better'n last year."

She held the dress in front of her belly, which wasn't showing yet. "It's beautiful, but I worry 'bout spendin' money on such things."

"The money's here, girl, and there ain't no end in sight. Go try it on."

* * *

Augusta was unsure how Cookie would feel about the baby. "Yer gonna be a mama?" She shook her head, grinning. "Oh, that poor baby." She leaned over and spoke to Augusta's belly. "Good luck, little baby, with a mama like ya got, but don't worry—ya got Aunt Cookie."

Cookie snapped to standing. "I won't be an aunt, I'll be a half-sister." She spoke to the baby again. "Ya got a sister older than yer mama."

Augusta and Cookie had store-bought dresses, and they didn't have to fret over what they could afford when they went into town for groceries. Augusta had never known that kind of financial freedom. She'd learned from her mother how to compare the money they had in their pocket and the list of items they needed, and shop carefully. Simon's farm was doing so well, she could buy flour and sugar whenever she needed them.

Simon was with her when she walked past a shop window and looked at a hat on display. "Ya like that?"

"I don't need a new hat, my old one looks just fine." She tucked a bit of hair along the edge of her hat.

"Our cotton's growin' thick an' high. I can afford that hat."

A month later Simon went off to the cotton mill with his biggest cotton crop yet, confident he'd be coming home with all the money he'd need to get through the winter in comfort. The year before, cotton had sold for twelve cents a bale, but that year his cotton sold for six cents a bale. Six cents would barely cover the cost of production. He lost money—a lot of money. On the way home he bought a bottle of whiskey and emptied it while swaying in the rocking chair in front of the fireplace, mumbling to himself.

* * *

Simon had been strapped for money before but he'd always managed to pay his way. Augusta watched him in the weeks that followed, fighting to keep from losing his farm. He sold every piece of equipment he had, old and new, and he and Augusta hand-planted the late-season crops. Simon took work wherever he could find it. He worked on other farms, road crews, and hotel kitchens, but he couldn't make up for the losses. Late one night, after a long day's work, he sat slouched in his chair, half-drunk again. "I shoulda saved up some. I shoulda kept livestock. I shoulda never planted cotton. I shoulda . . ." His voice dribbled off into drunken slumber.

Augusta thought his drinking wasn't helping anything, but kept that to herself. Cookie argued when her father left another empty whiskey bottle on the floor. The first time he hit his daughter, Augusta could see the shock in Cookie's eyes. After that, Cookie stood up to him often, and if Augusta defended her friend she got the back of Simon's hand. "Ya'll take yer husband's side or get more'n that fer yer trouble."

Cookie whispered, "Don't argue with him, Augie, he's drunk."

Later, when they were alone in the garden, Augusta asked, "Why d'ya pick fights with him like that when ya know he's gonna hit ya?"

"I just don't care anymore. He didn't used to be like this. He drank a bunch after Mama died, but only fer a couple days."

Augusta wiped her hands on her feed-sack dress. "Do ya think it's my fault, that yer papa shouldn't a married me?"

"Oh no, Augie, it's nothin' like that. Right after he married ya things was goin' good. Cotton was growin' thick an' sellin' high. But the lumber company gave cotton seed to almost ever' farmer 'round here. Yer papa said that when ever'body planted the same crop things'd go bust, an' that's why he planted strawberries an' apples, an' kept livestock. Yer papa was right. When my papa lost the tractor an' harvester, this place went to hell in a hurry, an' he went with it. This ain't yer fault."

Chapter Nine

Goodbye

Augusta walked past the vegetable garden toward her empty-looking childhood home. The gray frame house had been painted the same color as the barn when Papa found a sale on paint that was used up north in some factory. The paint had come in a big metal barrel, and when the barn, milk house, and machine shed were all painted, he had enough left to paint the house. Mama had wanted the house to be white, but she couldn't argue with paint that was there for the taking.

Augusta looked at the dark windows on the gray house, remembering the days the family had worked together, painting everything the same drab color. She was almost in tears, thinking no one was home, when she saw her mother holding the screen door open. Augusta was in her mother's arms, crying like a child, and her mother guided her to a chair. "Now, Augusta, ya need ta dry those tears an' start actin' like a grown-up. Yer gonna be a mama soon."

Augusta cupped her hands around the growing belly beneath her feed-sack dress. "I don't wanna have this baby without ya, Mama."

"Ya'll be havin' that baby wherever ya are, with or without me. Ya've seen enough birthin' to know what's comin'. Women have been having babies since the beginning a time, it's part a nature, like breathin'."

Augusta wiped tears from her cheeks. "But Simon's movin' us ta Detroit. We don't know nobody up there, an' Yankees're gonna laugh at the way we talk."

Her mother sat across the table from her. "Simon's yer husband, an' he's got a job up there. That's where ya'll be raisin' that baby."

"But Mama . . ."

Being in the familiar kitchen, listening to her mother's voice was calming. Augusta flashed on a morning years before, when Mama declared, "Walking into this yellow kitchen ever' mornin' feels like a second sunrise." Papa, pouring his coffee, said, "Looks more like a big egg yolk ta me."

Since then Augusta had felt it too, even on rainy mornings—the kitchen felt like a sunny day. The day she came to say goodbye, she resented the sunny color. Her mother stood and reached deep into a cupboard, pulled out a lemon, and cut it, squeezing each half into a glass. She added big spoonfuls of sugar, and they carried their glasses to the hand pump in the yard. Back in the kitchen, they sat stirring their drinks.

Lemons were special. They rarely ate anything that didn't grow on the farm. Augusta's mother must have traded an apple-rhubarb pie for lemons recently. The closest farm that grew such a treat was in Porter Valley, not close by. Had Mama gotten a lemon just for her? She wanted that to be true, but didn't ask.

Mama took a sip of lemonade and asked with a smile, "So, what's goin' on with Clara?"

"Simon told Cookie she should marry Albert, but she don't want that. She went ta a dance with him once and didn't like him much."

"Augusta, gettin' what you want don't usually happen."

Augusta replied, "Miss Carpenter helped Cookie find a job cleanin' at a boardin' house, and she'll be livin' in another boardin' house. Simon says she'll be cleanin' up after men she don't know an' livin' with a bunch a old maids."

Augusta worried about her friend, but couldn't help wondering what it would be like to make her own choices, to just look after herself. She thought it might be lonely, but she still wondered, then she touched her bulging tummy.

"Mama, he's been drinkin' more and more."

"He's a man who just lost the farm he worked on all his life. He'll go back ta his ornery old self when he can feed an' take care a his family. Men're like that."

"But he's so mean when he drinks."

Mama leaned back in her chair. "He's a good man who's havin' a hard time. You're his wife an' you can outlast this rough patch."

"But Mama, his rough patches are runnin' all together."

"He's your husband an' you have an obligation till ya die. Nobody gets what they want. Ya'd best learn ta want what ya get."

They finished their lemonade and were standing on the porch saying their goodbyes when Joseph walked out of the barn. Mama asked, "What ya doin' out there, boy?"

He wiped his hands on a greasy rag. "Papa told me ta clean up that old sawmill table an' sharpen an' polish the

blades. Thinks he could sell 'em ta that guy over in Porter."
Joseph walked toward them as he talked. He was at the
porch steps when Mama took Augusta by the shoulders and
said, "You'd best be gettin' home."

Then she looked at Joseph. "Walk yer sister ta the creek
an' say yer goodbyes along the way."

Augusta grabbed her mother's hands. "What about Papa?"

Mama pulled her hands free and patted her daughter's
arm. "Yer papa won't be back till dark, an' ya should be home
long fore that. Now, get goin', gir—woman."

Joseph guided her toward the creek in relative silence.
They had a lot to say, but neither knew how to start. Augusta
finally said, "I wanted ta say goodbye ta Papa. Is he out in
the field somewhere? I wanna see him."

"He ain't in any field, he's meetin' with Simon."

"What's he doin' with Simon?"

"I ain't sure, but I think he's tryin' ta get him ta treat ya
better. I know what I'd say."

Tears raced down her cheeks. At the creek Augusta
grabbed Joseph in a bear hug and he hugged back like he
never had before. Joseph didn't speak; he turned her toward
Simon's farm and gave her a gentle push. She took a couple
of steps, and when she looked back over her shoulder, Joseph
was disappearing into the woods.

* * *

Augusta was crumpled between all the possessions they
could fit into their half of the pickup truck bed. Simon had
agreed to pay for half of the gas in exchange for the ride. The
other half contained the household items of people she'd

never met; a woman and two children wedged in among them.

The truck pulled away from the house Augusta had begun to call home. In two years she'd discovered a happiness she'd never guessed at, followed by an aching sadness these last few weeks as her husband turned into a man she didn't recognize. She leaned back against a rolled-up rug and let her gaze drift to the mountaintops, wondering where she was going and whether she'd ever see the Ozarks again.

Augusta tried to stand, to find a more comfortable position, and nearly fell over when the truck hit another bump. The tired-eyed woman on the other side of the truck handed a heavy wool blanket to her son and pointed at Augusta. The boy crawled over boxes and a couple of chairs to hand her the worn woolen treasure. Augusta smiled at the boy. "Thank ya." She looked to his mother and gave a nod. The tired eyes dipped and looked away.

Augusta leaned back again against the rug, now padded with the blanket, and watched the mountains bobbing with the motion of the truck. She wanted to watch them slowly disappear, but fell asleep. When she woke, the ground around them was flat and the sky as gray and empty as she felt.

It was four days in that truck from Arkansas to Detroit, and the woman never said a word except to her husband and children, and she didn't say much to them. When they stopped for gas the woman and her two boys jumped out. The oldest one held out his hand to help Augusta down. Her baby wasn't close to coming, but she thought the rough roads were about to shake it loose.

It was late November, the weather getting colder and

grayer as they neared Detroit. Augusta was glad for the comfort of the wool blanket over her feed-sack dress. Simon had sold her fancy pregnancy dress. "Ya ain't gonna need a fine dress like this." Augusta didn't think she'd needed it to start with.

After days on the road the truck stopped with a finality that said they'd reached their destination. The men came around and helped the women down, the children clambering behind them. They stood in a muddy field with tall brick buildings all around them. The air reeked, and Augusta asked, "What's that smell?"

Simon stood with his hands on his hips. "That's the smell of a new life."

Augusta wondered what kind of new life came with such a stench. Sam, the man who owned the truck, explained, "That's the smell a the metal stampin' plant."

The dingy sky full of acrid smells made Augusta's stomach turn, and she started to shake. When she tried to stop, she shook harder. *What is wrong with me?* The silent woman took her elbow, led her to sit on the truck's running board, and draped the blanket around her. Augusta sat bundled against a chill that came from within. She heard the men talking about where to go from there. Learning they didn't have a plan beyond getting to Detroit didn't ease her fears.

They spent their first night in a field between huge factories, the first such buildings Augusta had ever seen. Their slab sides, full of dark little windows, looked sinister as daylight faded and the cold settled around their odd camp. She remained curled in her blanket until the silent woman led her to a table and chairs near a tiny fire on the ground. The men were gathering wood, and Augusta realized she'd be sleeping in the truck again. *This is my welcome to Detroit.* She looked around at the menacing buildings silhouetted against the murky sky. *Oh, Mama, what is going to happen to my baby?*

Chapter Ten

What's a Tenement?

S imon and Sam did have jobs lined up, but they all lived in the truck until the police showed up and told them they had to move on. The family that seldom spoke, who continued to be a mystery to Augusta, silently piled into the truck with her. After all that time, she still didn't know their names. She only knew Sam's name because that's what Simon called him. The truck rattled onto the road and Augusta heard one of the policemen say, "Stupid hillbillies."

Simon said they had a place in a tenement, and Augusta wondered why they hadn't moved there before. She didn't know what a tenement was and didn't ask, feeling like a stupid hillbilly. Their tenement was a large brick building between other large brick buildings. Their apartment was small and dim, and they barely got their furniture and boxes off the truck and inside when Simon left. "I gotta be ta work by eleven."

Sam's truck rattled back to pick him up. Simon got into the truck and Augusta gathered the strength to ask, "Who goes ta work in the middle a the night?"

Sam laughed and Simon set his hand on her arm.

"Factories go 'round the clock up here, an' we been moved ta the midnight shift. I'll be home 'bout seven in the mornin'."

Sam leaned forward, speaking through the passenger window, "Keep yer door locked. I hear there's a lotta thievin' 'round here." They drove away, leaving her in the dark not believing a word they'd said.

Augusta walked alone back up the three flights to her new home. But when she reached the landing on the third floor she was unsure which of the five doors was theirs. There were numbers on four of the doors, and she thought hers was 3A4, but couldn't be certain. She tentatively opened the door and was relieved to see her grandmother's rocking chair. She looked at the door Sam had said led to their john. Along the road from Arkansas the gas stations called them restrooms, but Sam always called it the john. Augusta wondered why, but never asked, even when Sam pointed to the door on the third-floor landing marked REST ROOM, and said, "Yer lucky ta have an indoor john, some places still have outhouses. Ya got it handy, right here."

She opened the handy door and gasped. It smelled worse than any outhouse she'd encountered. There were two stalls without doors, with porcelain toilets like the ones she'd seen in stores and movie theaters. She knew they were supposed to be white, but they were so dirty they could have been any color beneath the filth. The lock on the door was broken, so she had to work fast.

Later, she sat in her grandmother's rocking chair surveying her new home. The room had a small window looking out at the brick wall of the next building. Lying among the boxes they'd brought with them were odds and ends of someone else's life. *The people who moved out must have left quickly—*

why else would they have left clothing and toys? The wall on Augusta's right had a porcelain sink next to a legged bathtub on a seven-inch platform. *Why'd they make a tub taller and harder to get into?*

The wall to her left had their only window, and next to that was a woodstove. At home, the men went into the forest and cut the wood they'd need for winter, then split and stacked it in a woodshed. Winters in Detroit were colder than Arkansas—where would they find wood and how would they store it? The stove sat on a thin slab of stone, with another slab leaning against the wall behind it, to keep the wall and floor from catching fire. There were sticks of firewood in the corner near the stove, but there wasn't much. The wall above the stove was soot covered.

Augusta wondered if it was soot from the stove that gave the walls a gray cast. She wasn't sure what color the walls had been painted long ago, but now they were varying shades of gray. The ceiling over the sink had been wallpapered, but the paper was falling away, dripping from the ceiling.

There was a second room, where their mattress lay on the floor. She kicked away the debris of people she'd never meet to clear a space around the mattress. In the wall between the two rooms was a door and a window, with barely enough room for both. *Is this some Yankee thing?*

She heard voices. Some distant, and she couldn't make out their words; others sounded like they were standing outside her door, speaking in normal tones, discussing something Jimmy was in trouble for doing, and she could hear every word. She thought she heard whispering. *Does it sound like whispers because they are rooms away, or are they whispering because they don't want to be heard?* She strained to hear something beyond the voices all around her, hoping to hear an owl call in the distance.

She wasn't going to be able to sleep with all the noise, so she started to clean. The previous tenants had left some Borax soap on the shelf above the sink. The single light bulb overhead provided enough light to clean by. *Dim light might be best for rooms like this.* The sink was her first target—she knew there was white porcelain in there somewhere.

She jumped when water came pouring from the faucet— she hadn't thought it would work. Why would someone leave this mess right where the water to clean it came out of the wall? She hadn't used much indoor plumbing, but she knew the water wasn't supposed to look like tea. After it ran for a minute or two it cleared, but still smelled funny. She filled a wash bucket and went to work.

* * *

When Simon came home she proudly showed him the product of her all-night cleaning campaign. He nodded and gave her a one-armed hug. "I'm just hungry an' tired. Can I look at all a this later?"

Augusta burst into tears. "I don't have nothin' ta feed ya. I got a little bag a flour, a little yeast, an' some sugar left, but nothin' else."

Simon hugged her again and whispered in her ear, "Sam an' I picked up food on the way home." He stood back and held out the big brown paper bag he'd been cradling in his other arm. "The markets in this town keep the same weird hours as the factories. I couldn't believe we could buy food at seven o'clock in the mornin'. The store keeper said he opens up fer an hour or so during shift change." Simon gestured toward the table. "Why don't we sit down at this shiny clean table an' have us some breakfast?"

He set the bag down and pulled out butter, milk, six eggs, four potatoes, and a small chicken. Augusta glanced at the icebox and Simon said, "Sam an' I're goin' ta get ice later. It'll be okay fer a couple hours. First, I need food an' sleep."

She started a fire in the stove with some bits of lumber from the pile that stood upright in the corner beside the stove. When the skillet was hot, she fried half a potato to go with their scrambled eggs.

"Sorry, we got no bread." Augusta served their first meal in their new home, but it wasn't much. They curled up together on the mattress Augusta had turned into a bed with blankets and pillows from the boxes they'd brought.

*　*　*

Augusta was awake and quietly sweeping up things she'd missed the night before when Simon looked at her through the window beside the bedroom door. "Ain't this the damndest thing ya ever seen?" He walked through the door beside the window and saw a bowl sitting on the table with a towel draped over it. "Ya makin' bread?"

"It won't be ready ta bake till tomorrow mornin'. I'll have ta do some figurin' with a new stove, but we should have bread for breakfast. That tiny bit a wood in the corner might do, but we're gonna need more."

"Sam an' I been figurin' on that."

They could smell someone else's bread baking nearby. Simon put on his jacket, which had been hanging on a hook near the door, and handed Augusta hers. "What say we go fer a walk."

They opened the door onto the third-floor landing and saw a woman and small child walk out of the john. Augusta had decided to call it a john because it was *not* a restroom. No one would want to rest in there for one more second than they had to. The woman looked young but tired. She wore a long, dark skirt and blouse that looked as tired as she did. The child was four or five, and Augusta couldn't tell whether it was a boy or girl. Eager to meet her neighbors, Augusta took a step toward them. "Hi, we're yer new neighbors."

The woman jumped back as though Augusta had slapped her. She pulled her child away and took short quick steps to the door diagonally across from theirs, 3C4, ushered the child in, and slammed the door.

Simon and Augusta looked at one another and shook their heads. On the stairs between the first and second floors they met another neighbor, an older man with graying hair and slouching shoulders. They stood to the side so he could pass on the narrow stairway, and as he neared, Simon said, "Mornin'."

The man walked by without looking at them, and mumbled, "Is it?"

Simon looked at his pocket watch. "I guess it ain't mornin' no more." They started down again and Simon said, "Friendly bunch, don't cha think?"

They stood on the tiny patch of ground between the porch and the alley. There was nothing green, not one blade of grass, to be found. It looked like someone had planted broken glass, bits of metal, and scraps of cloth, which poked out of the soil like a spring crop.

Augusta looked at the rows of rope clotheslines running from building to building overhead, like a giant spider's web with bits of cloth stuck in it. She could barely see the sky through the flapping clothes.

Simon took her hand and they passed through a fallen gate to look up and down the alley. The rutted lane between crowded buildings was lined with trash cans and debris. Augusta jumped when a rat scurried from behind the trash can near her feet. Simon laughed. "I think that's who was dancing in our walls last night."

Augusta had noticed the scritch-scratch of animals in the walls after the voices around them settled to near silence, but she'd thought Simon was asleep because the loudest scramblings had been next to his head. She looked at the tail still visible beside the metal can. "I ain't never seen a rat so big."

"They grow big as dogs up here. I wonder if we could train one ta run all the others off. A guy at the plant said he had a rat terrier that would hunt an' kill rats all day long. Said he ain't got no rats in his place, the dog scared 'em off."

Augusta watched the rat's long, hairless tail slide behind the trash can.

"Let's go this way." He pulled her hand back toward their building. They couldn't walk side by side in the narrow space between buildings, so he held his hand back and she walked behind, looking up at the metalwork above their heads that almost touched both walls. "That's the fire escape," Simon explained.

Augusta pulled her hand away and gaped at the four stories of metal above her. "How do ya git down from up there?"

"Ya see that ladder?" Simon pointed just above the first-floor windows. "When yer up there, ya can push it down an' climb down. They can't leave the ladder down, or people'd be crawling in our window like the rats in the wall."

He took her hand and led her to the front of the building, which opened on a cobbled street. There were more people here, and when Augusta said hello to a woman walking past, she nodded but didn't speak.

Simon squeezed her hand. "We gotta get ya a dress."

Augusta looked at her tummy, where her feed-sack dress stood out. Was Simon embarrassed to be walking with her? She decided it didn't make any difference what she was wearing; no one looked at her.

A couple approached from the left and she tried again. "Howdy."

They pulled closer together and crossed the cobbled street like they were trying to get away from her. "Strangers don't talk much up here, not like down home." Simon took her hand again.

"How do they get ta be friends if they don't talk?" Augusta asked.

"I guess they ain't lookin' fer friends, they just wanna be left alone."

Alone. That's how Augusta was feeling. Simon held her hand, but it didn't make her feel less alone in this noisy, smelly place. There were voices bouncing off the buildings all around them, shouting and talking to each other, but not to her. She could smell food cooking. She recognized the fragrances of bread baking and chicken roasting, but there were spices and meat smells that were new to her.

The front of their building didn't look much different

from the back, aside from a bigger door and wider porch steps. The bare soil between the building and the road had fewer bits of glass and metal, but it was packed earth with no sign of life. She hadn't realized how much life Arkansas soil contained and longed to see something soft and green. She looked up at the clotheslines weaving back and forth above the street. "They hang laundry ever'where."

They walked down the street together, passing people who did not see them. She tried not to, but had to at least nod. She may as well have been nodding to the few stark trees they passed.

"Did ya just tip yer head ta that tree?"

"Well, nobody else notices."

"We'll make friends. We just need ta adjust ta them, an' wait till they're ready. Like trainin' a horse ta plow. Let 'em get used ta the harness an' walk 'em 'round the plow till they ain't bothered by it. Some horses take longer'n others."

Augusta thought of Sam's silent wife. She smiled, thinking that woman had found a place where people rarely spoke to one another, just the right place for her.

Chapter Eleven

Agata

The aroma of roasting chicken made their dingy rooms feel more like home, but that feeling disappeared as the fragrance dissipated. Simon left for work at ten p.m., and Augusta felt more alone than the night before. Simon and Sam had brought ice for the icebox and more wood for the stove that afternoon. She'd never used two-by-fours and wood planks to cook with—it wasn't exactly firewood, but it leaned nicely in the corner.

Augusta sat in her grandmother's rocking chair with the smells of dinner settling around her. *I have to get used to this place. This is where I live.* She cupped her hands around her growing belly. "I gotta make this a home fer ya."

During the day the buildings bubbled with other people's lives, their voices, smells of their cooking, and Augusta felt more alone hearing and smelling what they would not share. Late at night it grew quiet. That's when quarrels could be heard, the sound bouncing off the brick walls like echoes in a canyon. On quieter nights she could hear the wind in the sad old tree in the yard behind the building next to theirs. The sound took her home to Arkansas, where she could walk in bare feet. No one walked in bare feet around here.

Simon brought her a dress the next day. It was a green floral pattern—not new, not too old, just a dress. "Where'd ya get this?"

"One a the guys at work gave it ta me. His wife wore it when she was pregnant."

Augusta didn't know why, but she didn't like that word. It didn't sound right to her. "With child," "in a family way," or "mother-to-be" all sounded better than "pregnant," which she thought sounded dirty.

Simon got his first paycheck and gave Augusta money for groceries. He told her the market was two blocks over and one block up. She wasn't sure what that meant, but he pointed left, then right, so she figured she could find it. She wore her new dress on her first walk to the market. She did feel better, wearing a dress like everyone else. She nodded as she passed a woman, who responded with, "Hello."

Augusta spun around. "Hi."

Agata was a lean Polish woman who spoke a broken English Augusta could barely understand. She caught some words, but the rest made no sense at all. Agata pointed at herself and said, loud and slow, "Ag-a-ta."

Augusta pointed at herself and said, "Au-gus-ta."

Agata laughed and said, "Same, same. Agata and Aug-us-ta. Same same."

Augusta had made her first city friend. When she took the trash out the next night, Agata waved from her window. She lived almost directly across the alley. Augusta was trying to get used to living with a street in front of her building and an alley that reeked of rot and rat urine in the back. Knowing that Agata lived just beyond that smell made it less bad.

* * *

Augusta heard a racket on the stairs, then a loud rapping on her door. She wasn't sure she should open it. "Who's there?"

"It's yer lovin' husband. Open up fore he tips over."

Her first thought was that he'd been drinking again, but when she opened the door Simon and Sam stood there holding two flat squares of wood between them. She threw the door open. "What's that?"

They charged into the room. "Pallets. Stuff comes ta the factory on wood pallets. They got no use fer em, so we can take 'em home."

Augusta was clearing a space near the woodstove for the pallets when Simon said, "Don't bother with that."

He went into the bedroom, tipped the mattress up, and set one pallet down. Sam set the other beside it. Simon tipped the mattress back down, and their bed sat a few inches taller. Simon reached into the open end of a pallet and pulled out some broken boards, like the kind leaning in the corner near the stove. "Lookie here." He sat on the mattress. "With any luck, we'll need a ladder ta get inta bed fore the snow falls. This here's our woodshed."

Sam looked around. "You got one a those inside windows."

Simon stood up. "What the hell's that about?"

"I guess they passed some law that ever' room had ta have a window, an' that window kills two birds with one rock. They din't say the window had ta go nowhere." Sam walked through the door beside the window and pointed to the window that opened to outside. "Then there was a new law 'bout windows that open outside. They call 'em tuberculosis windows—see how the plaster's all busted up 'round the window? They added that one then." He leaned out the window. "Ya got yer own clothesline too. That's handy."

Augusta thought it looked about as handy as the john. "Why do they call 'em tuberculosis windows?" Augusta wasn't sure what tuberculosis was, but she knew it wasn't good.

"I guess gettin' air in here helps keep people from gettin' sick."

"Sam, how d'ya know so much 'bout all this?" Simon was setting wood up in the corner near the stove. "Ya live in a house, not a tenement."

"I got a neighbor from Alabama just itchin' ta talk ta anybody who'll listen. He could talk the leg off a that chair."

After Sam left Augusta asked, "How come they live in a house an' we live here?"

"They live in a shack down by the river, an' it ain't much. They got one outhouse an' an outside hand pump for water for about four shacks. I think we got it better here."

Simon put his hands on her shoulders. "I know this place ain't much, but if I can save some money I'll get us a little house somewhere. It'll be a lot better'n those shacks by the river."

Augusta wasn't feeling reassured until he gave her a hug.

* * *

Her first laundry day taught Augusta why the bathtub was on top of a step. It was the perfect level to do laundry. She could run water into a bucket in the sink, warm it over the stove, and pour it into the tub. The clothes could slosh in the water and she could use her washboard without bending forward much. Her belly appreciated that feature. Scrubbing a pair of Simon's work pants on the washboard, she announced to the empty room. "Now, *this* is handy."

When she pulled the plug to empty the tub, water rushed down the drain and she wondered where it was all going. She imagined a basement full of water far below. She knew that wasn't right, but she thought of it every time she heard water being sucked down the drain.

She stretched out the window and hung the wet clothes on the line, rolling the clothesline out over the alley. One day, while Augusta was hanging laundry, the woman in the apartment above dropped a shirt and it landed on the line right in front of her. She grabbed it before it could fall to the ground, and looked up. The woman waved, pulled back from her window, and returned, letting down a rope with a hook attached.

"Put on hook, please." She spoke with an accent Augusta didn't recognize.

She put the shirt carefully on the hook and looked up. "Here ya go."

Augusta watched the woman retrieve her shirt, then called up to her. "I'm Augusta, in 3A4."

The woman pulled back into her apartment and closed her window. Augusta knew she was in 4A4, and that she used bleach on her whites, but that was all she would ever know.

She'd learned what the numbers on the apartment doors meant. 3A4 indicated that she lived on the third floor, apartment A, in tower 4. The building had four towers, each tower had its own stairway, and each floor had four apartments, A through D, and a john. Sixteen families lived in tower four, and sixty-four families lived in their building. No wonder there was always laundry hanging.

Augusta couldn't believe she was getting used to the noises and smells. She still tried to talk to people. She didn't think she'd ever get used to people ignoring one another.

*   *   *

Although stamps cost two cents, Augusta wrote her family as soon as she could spare them, using a pencil she found on the street. Their meat came wrapped in brown paper, and she'd save the crisp edges to fold into an envelope held together with flour-and-water paste. She used another piece of the paper to write her letters. She told her family about their tenement, but not too much. Mama was glad Simon had a job and wasn't drinking. Joseph asked more specific questions: How big is Detroit? How big is the factory? What kind of cars does Simon work on?

She loved hearing from them. Mama wrote and Joseph wrote, and told her what Papa was doing on the farm. Those words made her miss them even more. She could almost smell the fresh-turned soil when Joseph wrote about spring plowing, and longed to set her bare feet in the soft cool earth. Closing her eyes, she could see the mountain views from the vegetable garden.

Her words about the tenement were careful; she didn't want to complain. Mama didn't probe, but Augusta thought she could tell tenement life was not good. Mama wrote things like, "Simon is making money and, if you're careful with your spending, you'll be able to move to a bigger place when your baby comes."

I thought I was being so happy when I wrote, but she can tell how I really feel. I'll be more careful in my next letter.

Chapter Twelve

My Baby

The morning Augusta's water broke, she stood in the alley and called up to Agata's window, the smell from the trash cans especially foul. Agata put her head out the window. "Come up, I make korek—" she tapped her forehead "—jam. I make strawberry jam."

Augusta's hands rested on her belly. "I think this baby's comin'."

Agata's head disappeared with a thud as she smacked it on the sash. Augusta reached around to the back of her own head. *That must have hurt.* Agata came down the two flights so fast, Augusta jumped at her presence. "Agata, did ya turn off the stove?"

She disappeared up two flights, turned off the stove, and was back before Augusta got to her porch steps. Agata tried to put her arm around Augusta's shoulders, but the width of the steps wouldn't allow it. Augusta held onto the railing and pulled herself up the stairs while Agata walked behind with her hands on Augusta's hips. "I do this so you not fall."

It was a long three flights to the room Augusta had prepared. She'd pulled the mattress to the floor and covered the wooden pallets with a couple of blankets. Agata asked, "Why you move mattress?"

"Agata, have ya ever seen a baby born?"

"No, in Poland babies come at the market." She laughed, Augusta didn't. "We don't take mattress away, we have cover."

"Did ya bring one with ya?"

"Okay, okay, I get pillow for your head."

Augusta had seen many births, animal and human. She knew women often screamed and cried, but animals rarely did more than moan during delivery. She'd decided years before that she would be strong and quiet. With her first contraction she thought of Bella and her many calves, but it didn't help at all. She knew now why women carried on the way they did—the pain was beyond what she'd imagined. She kept trying not to make noise but it didn't work. She thought she'd be calm and quiet during the next contraction, but she wasn't. Agata wiped her brow and spoke to her, but she didn't feel much like talking.

The first cry from her baby pushed everything else to the background. She wanted to see it, to count its fingers and toes. Agata was talking to the baby. "You are sweet little girl." She looked at Augusta. "It is girl, perfect little girl."

Augusta sat in a chair holding the eighth wonder of the world swaddled in one of Simon's shirts. Agata cleaned up, set the mattress back in place, and made up the bed again. Augusta couldn't believe how strong her daughter was, gripping her little finger like a tiny pink vise.

As she set things right, Agata kept up a steady flow of chatter. "I never see such a thing. You never speak one word, never noise, just push the baby."

"Agata, what're ya talkin' 'bout? I screamed like a cat with its tail in a wringer."

"No, no words, no scream."

Augusta leaned back and closed her eyes. *That's how they do it. All those animals I thought were being so strong were screaming in their heads. No, I'd rather think they were that strong. The look in Bella's eyes was not a scream. I was sure I'd been yelling.*

Agata yammered on as she cleaned the apartment and found some chicken to make a salad for when Simon came home. "What you name your baby?"

"We decided on Thelma if it's a girl. That's Simon's mama's name."

"Thelma is pretty name. I like. Simon have chicken salad in icebox, not much, but good."

"That's perfect, Agata. I think I need ta rest awhile."

"You sleep. Simon home in two hours. I come tomorrow."

Alone with her baby as dusk came, Augusta looked at her sweet girl and knew she wouldn't be lonely anymore.

* * *

Augusta had seen many babies, but hers was different. Thelma's tiny hands and feet were a marvel, and the first time she laughed Augusta's heart sang. Simon made a wooden crib from pallet boards, sanding the rough wood smooth so his little girl wouldn't get splinters. He brought home a tiny blanket the day after Thelma was born. "Sam's wife sent this for us." He didn't know the wife's name, either.

Augusta went about the job of homemaker in their two-room apartment as though it were the home she'd always dreamed of. She made makeshift curtains for their only exterior window and dug out some doilies she'd crocheted under her mother's supervision. She hadn't bothered with them before, thinking they wouldn't live there long. She removed the wrapping she'd placed around a green vase her mother had given her as a wedding gift, and carried it to the window, remembering the day her mother gave it to her. The light reflecting against the glass brought feelings she needed to repress. *Don't cry, Augusta, put that doily in the middle of your table. Make this place your home.*

She found a shovel, rake, and broom under the back porch, and used these ragged tools to clean up the dirt in their tiny yard, using her hands to sift through years of debris. There were pieces of bottle and bottle caps, metal pieces of all shapes and sizes, and bits of fabric from clothing that had been cast aside. *They use this place like a garbage dump.* She was at this task when Simon came home.

"What ya doin' there, girl?"

"When Thelma's ready ta crawl an' walk, I want a place fer her that ain't full a glass an' nails." She looked at her daughter nestled in a blanket set on an upside-down garbage can lid.

"So ya put our little girl in a trash can?"

"It's clean, an' I filled it with soft dirt with no junk in it. I made a nest an' she's sleepin' while I work."

"I'm gonna go sleep a bit. Changin' from midnights to mornin's is hard. I wish they wouldn't keep switchin' us 'round like that."

Augusta kept sorting through the dirt until she was sure Simon was awake again. The dirt patch was four feet wide and the length of the building. It was going to take days to clean up the mess. They ate lunch together, then Simon said he had some work to do and left. He hadn't been drinking since they got to Detroit, but whenever he walked off without explanation she worried.

She'd browned the meat and was putting the stew on to simmer when she heard noise in the yard where she'd been working. She craned her head out the window, but couldn't see more than the building next door. "Come on, Thelma, we gotta find out who's doin' what back there." The space of dirt behind their building belonged to all the people in the tenement. She hoped others might see her cleaning it up and lend a hand, but thought it more likely that someone might sabotage her efforts.

She stopped short when she stepped onto the porch. Simon and Sam were repairing the tattered fence that stood along the edge of the alley, and had rehung the gate. They smiled at Augusta as she walked down the steps, and Simon said, "If yer gonna clean this mess up, I guess we can put this piece a crap back together."

Thelma gurgled in Augusta's arms. "Yer papa's makin' space fer ya ta grow up in."

Months whirled past with little change. Simon went to work and came home, and Augusta adjusted to her home in what she thought of as a beehive, where the bees didn't like each other much. She made their two rooms as comfortable as she could, and she and Simon became comfortable again, laughing at Thelma's first steps and first words, and sometimes dreaming about a brighter future.

"Ya know, Augie (he called her Augie when he was in a loving mood), if we're careful with our money an' save up, we could buy a little house. Not too far away, but nicer'n here."

She loved when he talked like that. She would love to

have a house. It wouldn't have to be much, just a place of their own with more than one window.

Chapter Thirteen

Friends

Augusta looked into her toddler's eyes. "Thelma, yer growin' so fast an' so pretty. I don't want nobody callin' ya no stupid hillbilly, an' yer mama ain't gonna be one neither."

Augusta sat straighter, cupping her hands around her growing belly. She closed her eyes and recited, "I do not want anybody"—she hesitated—"anyone calling you a stupid hillbilly, and your mama is not"—*should it be isn't?*—"your mama isn't going to be one neither."

Thelma stood in front of her, holding a doll Simon had made, the kind Augusta had grown up with. "I hope you got a little brother coming here, cuz—because—your papa wants a son."

Thelma held out her arms and Augusta lifted her to her knee. "There ain't—there isn't—much room for you on my lap anymore. Your little brother or sister is coming soon."

She heard Simon's footsteps on the stairway, and set Thelma down to unlock the door. He didn't like having to use his key, but he also didn't like her leaving the door unlocked. On days she didn't unlock the door before he got there, she'd hear him swearing at the key or the lock or the doorknob—she wasn't sure which he was mad at.

Simon stepped through the door saying, "Ya'll had this locked, din't cha?"

"I heard you coming."

"How'd ya' know it was me?"

"I recognized your walk."

"Where'd ya' get a word like 'reconize'? Has that Edith been fillin' ya with Yankee crap again?" He hung his hat and coat on a peg near the door.

"She knows I don't like being called no stupid hillbilly." Augusta stood her ground. "She said if I talk like 'em, they won't know." She rehearsed in her head, *being called a hillbilly*. Edith told her she should stop putting the word "stupid" in there, because she wasn't.

"Ya ashamed a bein' from the Ozarks? Ashamed a bein' the wife a a stupid hillbilly? That talk ain't gonna make ya one a them." He threw Thelma's doll on the floor. "Is dinner ready or am I gonna starve ta death?"

She smiled as she stirred the goulash Edith had taught her to make. Thelma clung to her skirt with one hand, the doll, rescued from the floor, with the other. Augusta didn't remind Simon that he used to call their evening meal supper and now called it dinner. He was changing too, he just didn't know it. He was mad a lot lately but he wasn't drinking, so she thought he must be working too hard. She consoled herself with the idea that he was just tired, and thought she'd rub his back after dinner.

Over a nearly silent meal, she thought about the friends she'd made. When Augusta met Agata, the two could barely understand one another. Agata loved children and Thelma loved her. Although they resorted to hand signals half the time, they'd become dear friends. They were in the market talking, signaling, and misunderstanding one another, when Edith stepped in. She understood Polish and English, although Augusta's southern drawl sometimes baffled her.

Edith reminded Augusta of her mother, though Edith wasn't quite as old and they didn't look alike; her mother was olive-skinned with black hair, and Edith had light-brown hair and eyes as green as Augusta had ever seen, like the eyes of a doll she'd once seen in a store window. But Edith's eyes were kind, like her mother's, and Edith had a bearing that attracted Augusta and Agata like chicks to a hen.

Agata introduced herself by tapping her chin while saying her name. She pointed to Augusta and butchered the pronunciation, saying afterward, "Same, same."

Edith explained that they had very different names. She said that the English version of Agata was Agatha and that, in Latin, it meant good and kind.

Augusta asked, "What's my name mean?"

"Augusta means majestic and grand. It was a name given to the daughters of Roman emperors."

Augusta asked, "How d'ya know all that?"

"My father was a college professor in Poland. He taught me Polish, English, Latin, and German."

Augusta was wondering how someone like Edith ended up in a tenement in Detroit when Agata asked, "What does Edith mean?"

Edith laughed. "My father taught English language, and history was his hobby. He chose my name from British history. In Latin my name means riches or blessed. My father's name was Edgar, and the English king Edgar the

Peaceful named his daughter Edith, and so did he."

Augusta asked, "What does Edgar mean?" She hadn't realized names had meanings.

"I don't remember." Augusta knew Edith remembered what her father's name meant, so she switched the conversation to the ripeness of the fruit displayed in front of them.

* * *

As they got to know one another, they shared stories about where they'd grown up. Agata's life had been simple, like Augusta's. She'd grown up on a farm, milking cows and caring for the house. She'd gone to a simple local school, but they couldn't figure out whether she'd received more or less education than Augusta. Their grade system was different.

Edith had gone on to university. She spoke of life growing up with a professor father. She always did her studies before she went out to play. She said her father was kind but strict, and pushed her to do well in school. She talked about books like they were friends, reminding Augusta of the two books on her mother's bureau. Why hadn't she ever read them, or even asked about them?

"I found a library." Edith's eyes glistened one afternoon. "It's only a few blocks away. It's not really a library, but a couple who love books are willing to share—they have so many books. I'm going to let them borrow this one." She held up a book with a battered black cover and words Augusta didn't understand. "They're from Poland and they don't have a copy of *Pan Tadeusz*. Do you want to come with me?" Augusta had never been in a library, and Agata's family hadn't had any books, except the ones she used in school.

"I can only read Polish," Agata said. "I'll stay here to watch Thelma. You two go without me."

Augusta was amazed at how quickly the neighborhood changed as they walked. Within a few blocks, they passed houses instead of tenements.

"That's where I live," Edith said, pointing to a lovely old house.

Augusta was amazed at how big her house was. "How do you take care of such a big house?"

"I rent an apartment in the back of the house. It's a lovely little space that opens onto the garden."

Augusta had noticed that Edith never mentioned parents or a husband, although she wore a wedding ring. "How can you afford rent in a house like this?"

"I tutor people in English, Latin, and Polish."

Before Augusta could ask another question, they arrived at a big wooden house, long ago painted white. The scrollwork over the front door reminded Augusta of the carvings her brother Joseph created on grave markers. The white-haired man who answered the door invited them in with the flourish of a bow and an extended right arm. "Welcome to our humble home."

"Thank you, James." Edith ushered Augusta through the door.

The entry hall was dim but welcoming, with more scrollwork on the stairway banister on their right. The archway on their left led to a parlor where every wall was a floor-to-ceiling bookcase. There were comfortable chairs around a table in the center of the room. Places to sit and read. Augusta didn't notice the white-haired woman, Rachel, until she stood up.

"Edith, it's so nice to see you. I see you brought a friend."

They sat and talked over tea and tiny cookies. Augusta got lost in talk of Poland and a few Polish words, but much of the talk was about books.

"I'm sorry your friend Agata didn't come. Do you think she would like a book?" James stood in preparation of finding the right book among the hundreds around them.

"She can only read Polish." Edith was looking through books on the other side of the room.

"That is easy to accommodate—this is one of my favorites from the old country." He handed a book to Edith.

"And what about you, Augusta, what sort of book would you like to borrow?"

"I didn't come to borrow a book. I haven't read anything since I got out of school, and I only went through eighth grade."

"Ah, something short and sweet."

Rachel walked to a wall of books and picked up a small green volume. Augusta was impressed that she knew where that particular book was.

Chapter Fourteen

Ivon

"I will help you with your new baby." Agata's English was getting better, or perhaps Augusta was getting used to her bad English. "I help with Thelma, now I help again."

Agata and her husband, David, were having no luck having their own baby, so Augusta felt guilty asking her friend to help with her second, but Agata insisted.

Augusta knew what was coming and was glad Agata would be with her. David told Agata to use a painter's cover for the bed, but Augusta pulled off the mattress and used blankets instead. When the contractions started she didn't yell, but she wanted to. The pain surprised her. Had she forgotten the pain or was this delivery harder? Her mama had told her, "If a woman didn't ferget birthin' pain she'd never have another."

She laughed at the memory of that conversation, and Agata reacted. "Now you scare me. You laugh and birth. You one crazy American."

"I was just thinkin' of my own mama. I didn't know how right she was sometim—ohhh . . ."

"Baby come, baby come."

The new baby was bundled in a blanket provided by Agata. "You are naming her Ivon—the Archer's Bow? Edith say Ivon will aim her life. She say Ivon good for boy or girl name. Ivon to balance Thelma's strong will. You name her Ivon still?"

"Yes, Agata, we name her Ivon still. Her papa wanted a boy, but she looks healthy and strong. Is Thelma still asleep?"

"Ya, she sleep like a baby. Now she have baby sister. They be friends, two happy girls. You are lucky to have such beautiful babies." Agata attempted to stifle a sniffle.

"Don't cry, Agata, you'll have a baby soon." Augusta filled the silence that followed. "Simon will be home soon. He's on the midnight shift again. I like it when he's on the midnight or afternoon shift. When he gets the early shift he has too much time in the afternoon to think about how much he hates his job, and I don't like to hear him talk like that. He says he puts one piece of metal on top of another piece of metal, over and over and over again. He says a monkey could do his job. When I talk to him about changing jobs, he gets mad and stops talking at all."

Agata spoke to the baby nestled next to Augusta. "Your daddy don't deserve two beautiful baby girls. He don't deserve a wife like your mama. Your mama deserves better than she gets."

"Please don't talk about Simon like that. He's my husband and my daughter's papa."

"Sorry. I don't mean to make you mad."

"I know." Augusta also knew it would be better if Agata was not there when Simon got home. Agata had everything set straight and was long gone when Augusta heard Simon swearing at his keys. *Why does he get so mad at something he knows is going to happen?*

* * *

Thelma was amazed by her little sister. Edith had told Augusta that sometimes the older child resents the new baby, but Thelma set her doll next to her sleeping sister. "I hope you two girls get along, cuz right now we're all we've got."

She watched them sleeping, Ivon in Thelma's homemade crib and Thelma in a dresser drawer Simon brought home as a bed for his growing daughter. "Someday, girls, we're gonna live in a house with more than one window, and you'll sleep in real beds."

Chapter Fifteen

Double Shifts

Ivon was almost a year old when Simon's work schedule changed again. He stopped riding back and forth with Sam because they were now on different shifts. He walked to the bus stop for the afternoon shift and didn't come back until after seven in the morning. "Are you working double shifts?"

Augusta had heard that sometimes happened. Agata's husband worked at the Ford plant and Simon worked for Dodge. Simon contended that the Dodge was a superior car, but Augusta thought that was only because he helped build them. Simon had been on the morning shift for over a month, but was in a bad mood so often, Augusta tried to keep herself and the little ones away from him. He hadn't struck Augusta since they got to Detroit, and he'd never touched the girls in anger, but his words struck like fists. She was relieved when he was on double shifts and only came home to sleep a few hours in the morning, then went back to work.

Augusta and Agata sat on the porch steps watching Thelma play in the dirt at their feet. Ivon slept in her mother's arms. "Simon's on double shifts again. I don't know how he can work so many hours, but he comes home in a bad mood almost every day. He's so tired."

"What you talking about?" Agata was making designs in the dirt for Thelma. "Both plants are down for changeover."

"What's changeover?" Augusta felt a knot in her stomach.

"When they change car designs, the plant closes until all the machines change over for the new model. It takes weeks, then they go back to work on a new car."

"When did changeover start?"

"Over a week ago."

Augusta felt cold and hot at the same time. *That's how long Simon has been on double shifts. If the plant was closed, where was he going?* She thought it might have something to do with drinking, but he hadn't come home drunk, just tired. The news weighed on her; it got in the way when she bathed Thelma, fed Ivon, made dinner. What was her husband doing all afternoon and night?

When Simon came home early the next day, Augusta was sitting at the table, but she didn't unlock the door. She listened to him swear at the lock and when he walked in, he asked, "Why din't ya unlock the door?"

"I didn't hear you coming."

He flopped into his chair and moaned, "This job is killin' me."

"What job is that?"

"Buildin' cars, woman. That's what I do, ya know."

Augusta had rehearsed what she wanted to say, but that went out the window as she began to speak. "Where are you building cars during changeover?"

Simon didn't move. Augusta could hear her own heartbeat.

His eyes were closed and she wondered if he was pretending to sleep. He didn't open his eyes as he spoke, "Who told ya 'bout changeover?"

"Most men around here work in factories."

"What *men* you been talkin' to?"

"The women know when their husbands stay home." She hesitated. "And they know when they don't."

Simon sat up and looked at her. "What's that mean?"

"You haven't told me where you've been when you *weren't* going to work."

"What's that mean?" He jumped up, knocking over his chair and rocking the table. Augusta saw her green vase teeter. She raced to catch it, but it rolled off the table and shattered. They both looked down at the green glass.

"I'm too tired for this shit." Simon stumbled into the next room and fell face-first onto the bed.

* * *

Agata had served breakfast to her husband David, so Augusta assumed the breakfast she was eating was Agata's. She ate what was in front of her, because it was there. She could barely remember sneaking past Simon's sleeping body with her daughters in her arms. She'd been standing in their tiny dirt yard holding Thelma's hand with Ivon cradled in her other arm when Agata appeared in her mist of tears and guided her to the kitchen she was now sitting in.

Thelma played with the toys she always found at Agata's and crawled around her mother's legs giggling. Agata paced the kitchen with Ivon in her arms, cooing and telling some sweet story in Polish to ears too young to understand. David stood and said, "I've got to get to work."

He kissed his wife and the baby in her arms. Thelma held out her hands and he picked her up, gave her a peck on the cheek, and whispered in her ear. He set a smiling Thelma on the floor and looked at Augusta, nodded, and left. As soon as he was out the door, Augusta turned to Agata. "I thought you said the factory was shut down, that there was no work."

"Some of the men in David's plant are painting houses during changeover, to make extra money."

For a brief moment Augusta allowed herself to think that Simon could be doing that, too, but in her heart she knew it wasn't true. He wouldn't hide working—and he was hiding something. But still, she could tell he hadn't been drinking. She sat at Agata's table and talked for hours. It took that long for the words to finally fall from her mouth. Even then, Augusta only said it because she thought her friend was about to. "Do you think he's seeing another woman?"

"Do you?"

Thelma was curled up in a chair in the corner, sound asleep, and Ivon slept in a wicker laundry basket. Augusta looked at them and didn't answer. She and Agata edged the topic, but their conversation didn't go back there. They talked about what Augusta might do if she were on her own, but the heart of the issue was left beating in the background.

Augusta watched from Agata's window, standing back so he wouldn't see her, as Simon came out the back door of their building and looked around the yard, then up and down the alley, and went back inside. She wondered if he would leave at his usual hour, even though he wasn't going to work.

When she crossed the alley later that afternoon, the light

slanted on the trash cans. She wasn't sure whether Simon would be there; he hadn't come out the back door again but sometimes he went through the warren of hallways to exit the front of the building. She carefully opened their door, grateful it was unlocked; she didn't have a key. Simon had told her she didn't need one. There was no one there.

She and the girls finished their day, and when Augusta put Thelma to bed she crawled in herself, wondering what would be coming the next day. The possible courses Augusta had discussed with Agata seemed out of the question once she was curled up waiting for sleep. Over Agata's table she'd thought Simon would beg her forgiveness, and was certain she could never accept his apology. Alone in the dark, listening to her daughters breathing as they slept, she knew she would give him another chance.

It was nearly seven in the morning when he returned. Augusta was still in bed when Simon unlocked the door without swearing. He flopped into his chair and sat looking at the ceiling. She left him there for a while, wondering what he would say and curious about what *she* might say. She stood in the doorway, wrapped in a blanket.

"What's her name?"

"Gloria." He didn't hesitate. He was ready to tell her what she wasn't sure she wanted to hear.

"Oh, glory be, her name is Gloria." *Why did I say that? I sound like a child.* Silence hung between them, giving her time to think of something intelligent to say, but Simon spoke first.

"I'm goin' back ta Arkansas, Gloria's comin' with me."

"So your gonna just get your things and walk on outta here?"

"I already took ever'thing I want." He stared at the ceiling.

Augusta leaned on the door frame. He had moved out. He was already gone.

Simon placed some money on the table. "This should get ya through fer a while." The door key sat on top of it like a paperweight.

She looked at the money and the key, and screamed, "You can't do this!" But no words came out. She tipped her head to the wooden door frame, staring at the money under the key—what he was willing to pay to leave her. She heard him shuffle to the door and when it clicked shut behind him her scream escaped in a raspy whisper. "Now what?"

* * *

The plan over Agata's table fell into place as if they'd plotted for months. Edith helped Augusta find a job as a waitress, and she was working within the week. She'd never worked in a restaurant, she'd rarely eaten in a restaurant, but she was enthusiastic and the restaurant owner, Mel, said she was a natural with the customers. Mel was built like a man who liked food. His short black hair looked melted onto his scalp by the heat of the kitchen, and his smile filled the restaurant like the fragrance of fresh coffee.

The customers liked her and she grew to like them. She hadn't realized there were people who ate in restaurants every day, the regulars. On her third day at work, her coworker, Jane, took Augusta aside during the slow part of the afternoon. "I don't want to make you mad or anything, but is that the only dress you've got?"

"Yes, it's the only one. I might be able to buy another

when I get paid."

The next day, Jane came in with two shopping bags full of dresses. "I've got three sisters and four aunts, between us we've got a wardrobe big enough for a movie set. Look through these and take what you want. I guessed your size, but I'm usually pretty good at that."

"I can't take this," Augusta said, astonished.

"They're all either outgrown—my sister's been gaining weight—or cast aside. They picked out what they wanted you to have. Their closets won't miss them."

That night Augusta tried on the seven dresses, and they all fit. There was a green dress with white collar and cuffs that reminded her of the first dress she'd selected at Ferguson's General Store, back in Arkansas.

She now had dresses in solids, florals, stripes, and checks. When she was through trying them on, she sat down and cried.

"What's wrong, Mama?" Thelma stood in front of her, almost in tears herself.

"Nothing's wrong, little girl. Things are just beginning to feel right."

On her first payday she wasn't sure what to do with her check. She asked Jane, "How do I turn this into money?"

Jane smiled. "Follow me. Mel pays us early, so we can walk to the bank and get it cashed before he opens up."

Augusta followed Jane's red hair, which bounced as she walked, wondering how she moved so fast in a skirt that tight. They walked through the bank's big brass doors and up to one of the women behind the counter, who said, "Hi, Jane."

"Hi, Bess."

Jane collected her money, and motioned behind her. "We got a new girl, her name's Augusta."

Augusta stepped up to the window and said, "I've never had a check before."

Bess smiled. "Well, let's hope you get a lot of them in the future. Just sign your name on the back the way it's written on the front."

She signed her name and Bess counted out her money. She'd never had so much money out in public and it made her nervous. The amount of money Simon left had seemed huge. Counting it out, she'd thought it enough for two months' rent and food, and hid it safely in an envelope in the flour canister, locked in her apartment. She looked at the wad of money now in her hand, out where other people could see it, and shoved the folded bills into her deepest pocket where Jane had told her to keep her tips.

* * *

Agata took care of the girls while Augusta worked. Augusta could afford rent and food, and had some left over every week. Agata didn't want to be paid, but Augusta and David came to an agreement.

Augusta didn't get much mail. Letters from Mama and Joseph had come often at first, but now were rare, so the big yellow envelope from Arkansas was a surprise. But when she opened it, she found legal papers. Simon had filed for divorce. She sat at the table, looking at it without seeing the words. She hadn't thought he was coming back, but now there was no doubt.

She showed the papers to one of her regulars at the

restaurant. Joe Warren, an attorney, read over the papers as he ate lunch. "He says that *you* left *him*."

"That's not so. He went back to Arkansas with his new girlfriend."

Joe pointed to the words she hadn't looked at. "He claims you abandoned the marriage."

"He left." She stared at the tabletop.

"Then you should fight this. You may be able to get some money out of it."

"He doesn't have any money, and I wouldn't want it if he did." She wiped her hands on her apron. "I don't want anything from him."

He turned the papers toward her. "Sign here, then write the date. I'll witness and you can put it in the mail."

She picked up his pen from the table and Joe shook his head. "I still think you should defend yourself."

She signed her name, saying, "I just want it done."

Chapter Sixteen

The Waitress

Carrying a full tray from the kitchen pass-through to the table in the far corner, Augusta shared greetings with her regulars as she deftly zigzagged the maze of tables. She liked her job, her co-workers, and her customers. She especially liked that she was able to pay rent and feed her family.

"I can't believe Ivon is walking already." Jim was a regular, one of the police officers who sat at the lunch counter, not the tables. "Our baby was born the day after yours, and he's still crawling."

"Don't you know that girls are just smarter and faster than boys?" Jane said as she clipped an order up for the kitchen.

"So, being smart and fast is the reason you're not married." Jim's partner Ben had a little crush on Jane.

"You betcha, mister." She wiggled a little more than usual as she walked away.

Augusta took the next tray to a table near the windows. Judith worked in an office across the street, so she was a lunch regular. "Did I hear that our little Thelma started school today?"

"No, she's too young for school. My friend Agata takes care of my girls when I work, and she's started taking in other children too. She's teaching them colors and numbers and such. She calls it Baby School, and started that officially today. I'm afraid Thelma is going to learn English with a Polish accent."

Augusta thought it was nice that Judith thought of her children as if they were her own. Marion, who worked with Judith and was sharing a table for lunch, had two boys at home. They shared stories as Augusta waited on them, and Augusta felt like she knew Marion's children, who she'd never met.

A lot of police officers ate lunch or dinner at the restaurant, depending on their shift; the precinct house was just around the corner. Patrick Delaney was a favorite of Augusta's. She thought his Irish accent was cute, and so was he. His partner, Tony Pastori, said, "Don't even look at that Mick. If you're looking for love, remember, Italians invented *amori*."

"That Wop doesn't know romance from rhubarb. Check out these wild Irish eyes." Patrick did have beautiful blue eyes.

Friendly banter went on with many of her customers, male and female. It felt like an extended family and made her workday race past. She usually came home feeling refreshed and eager to spend a few hours with her girls.

"Augusta, that guy's making a pass at you." Jane was rinsing dishes at the sink.

"No, he's not." Augusta picked up her order and walked off.

Jane grabbed a tray and caught up with her. "He certainly is. You ignore every guy who even looks at you."

Augusta was relieved to get to her table and deliver the orders. She had to admit, she liked being noticed, but her job was to raise her family and she didn't want to take a chance on anything or anyone that might get in the way.

"Augusta, if you don't wake up and look around, you're going to end up alone," Jane said, beside her at the pass-through.

"I'm not alone. I have a family and I'm comfortable the way things are."

"Comfortable isn't happy. Happy is something else altogether."

"Being comfortable makes me happy."

* * *

He had blond hair and blue eyes, like Patrick, but there was something else about him. He ordered lunch like any other customer, but he winked at Augusta when he paid his bill, and she blushed. It wasn't the first wink she'd gotten, but she was always surprised by them.

After he left, Jane moved up next to her. "Watch out for that one."

"Do you know him?"

"Never saw him before, but I know the type. Watch out, girl."

Ottis became a regular, and even when he sat at Jane's tables, Augusta took his order. Their flirting was obvious and, for the first time, she heard a complaint from Mel. "Augusta, you got more than one customer, you know. Don't forget you got a job to do here."

Ottis had a job with Ford, handling sales and licensing

for dealerships. Augusta wasn't certain what that meant, but she did know he was happy, and she was happy when he was around. When he asked if she would see a movie with him, she blurted, "I have two little girls at home—I can't just go out like that."

He hesitated, but not for long. "Bring them along. There's a cartoon matinee every weekend at the Bijou. You say the word, and I'll take all of us for a movie, and we'll stop for ice cream afterward."

That was their first date. Augusta was afraid the girls might be too young—Thelma was nine, Ivon seven. But they sat through *Snow White*, eating popcorn and sharing a Coca-Cola with their mother. Ivon only had to go to the bathroom once.

When they settled into their seats, Ottis leaned over and asked, "Do you know what the word Bijou means?"

"Jewel." She wondered if she should have let him tell her what it meant, but it was too late.

His lips were inches from her ear. "You're the brightest jewel here." She wondered how many women he'd said that to. She wondered if she should tell him a bijou was a tiny, delicate jewel. *I'm definitely not tiny or delicate. Shut up, woman, he's holding your hand.*

There were picnics, matinees, and walks in the park. Agata occasionally babysat so they could go out for dinner and see a grown-up movie. The first time they went to a party together Augusta was surprised by how much Ottis drank. *Oh no, oh no, not another drinker.* But when he drank it made him happier, even silly. He wasn't mean, like Simon. Ottis only drank at parties or had a beer or two at a picnic. She was unlikely to find a man who didn't drink at all; a happy drinker was the best she could hope for.

Ottis taught Augusta to drive a car. They practiced on Belle Isle, where the park traffic moved slowly and the streets were mostly one-way. When she felt confident on the island, she drove over the bridge and into the city, but didn't get far. She pulled into the first parking space she found. "This is harder than I thought." Her hands were shaking.

Ottis leaned over and kissed her cheek. "You can do this. Let's just drive around the block."

When they returned to the same corner, he said, "Now let's do two blocks."

She thought of her brother Joseph's talent for all things mechanical as she wrote a long letter about learning to drive. Someday, she'd drive her family to Arkansas. It would be a while, though. She didn't want to see Simon anytime soon.

When Augusta told Tony she was learning to drive, he said, "Patty, we need to warn everyone on traffic patrol." To Augusta, he said, "Remember, you're not driving a team of mules."

"Watch out, boys, you're talking about my girlfriend," Ottis said as he walked in. He was picking her up after work almost every day now.

"You're letting her learn to drive in that Buick out front?" Patrick stared at the shiny machine at the curb.

"Yep, that's my car."

"I'm ready." Augusta was tying her headscarf, with her purse clamped under her right elbow.

Patrick and Tony walked them to the car. Patrick ran his hand along the fender, then opened the door for Augusta, looking in at the interior. "This is a nice car."

Tony was wiping crust from the hood ornament with his

handkerchief. "Some bird was not showing this vehicle the respect it deserves."

"What do you guys drive?" Ottis puffed up with the compliments.

"I've got an old Model T." Patrick was patting the chrome sideview mirror.

"I've got three kids and a pocketful of bus and streetcar tokens," Tony said, rattling his pocket.

They were pulling away from the curb when Ottis said, "They seem like nice guys."

* * *

Ottis caught her off guard when he asked her to marry him, but she said yes without a qualm. The civil ceremony took place a few weeks later. Ottis had an apartment close to the restaurant, which was nicer than her tenement, but Ottis thought it too small. They found a little house to rent in Hamtramck, and Augusta was reminded of Simon's promises. It was a small house, but it was a castle compared to where she'd been living.

Their new home was white with a front porch and a chair on either side of the door. Ottis walked her into a living room with soft carpeting, a sofa, chairs, tables, and lamps. "It comes furnished," he said, opening one of the bedroom doors. "This'll be our room."

She peeked into a room with two windows, a double bed, two dressers—one low, one high—and a wardrobe. All the clothes she'd ever owned wouldn't fill all that space. Ottis guided her to the next door. "The girls can share this room." The room had one window between two small beds, plus a dresser and wardrobe. She walked in and turned around. Her girls had never had so much space for themselves.

They walked down the hall toward the kitchen, turned, and walked through an arched doorway on the right, which opened into a dining room. Augusta had never been in a house that had a separate room for eating. The home she'd grown up in had a table in the kitchen. She imagined sitting at this new table, looking out the window as they ate. The room was filled with a shiny wooden table, eight chairs, and a sideboard. She'd have to prepare a special meal to serve in such a space.

The door opposite the dining room led to a bathroom. The white porcelain toilet, sink, and tub gleamed. This was definitely not a john, or even a restroom. Ottis pulled a curtain that hung on a rod around the tub. "We have a big water heater, so you can take a bath or shower whenever you want." Augusta had never had a shower, but she didn't have much time to think about that; her tour guide was beckoning.

She stopped at the kitchen door. The walls were sunrise yellow, the color taking her back to Arkansas—she couldn't believe she had her own kitchen, and it was yellow. "Come on in here." Ottis stood in the middle of the room.

"We have a Frigidaire," he said, pointing to a white box with a whirring metal hatbox on top. He opened the thick door and pointed to what looked like a breadbox in the upper right-hand corner. "You can make your own ice, right here."

Ottis skittered to the stove. "You've got an electric stove. No wood, no gas, just push this button and the coils heat up. You got three burners, and turn this knob to turn on the oven." He opened the door on a dark space with two metal shelves.

While Augusta gaped at the oven, Ottis moved on to the sink. "We've got hot and cold water, no more heating water on the stove." There was a window over the sink revealing a backyard with a lawn and a tree. On the right side of the room was a table with six chairs adjacent to a big window. "So many windows . . ." Augusta exclaimed. She'd missed windows. She sat at the table and looked at the house next door. There was so much space between them. She looked down at the table. "Why would we need two places to eat?"

"The civilized world has an eat-in kitchen for breakfast and lunch, and a dining room for dinner and guests." *Ottis is trying to civilize me.* He took her hand and guided her toward the door beside the sink. She looked down at the surface they were walking on and Ottis stopped, like any good salesman. "Linoleum. It's the latest thing. You can spill milk or drop eggs on it, and just wipe it up."

He dragged her through the door onto a big back porch overlooking a green backyard. There was room to plant a garden. They had a kitchen, dining room, living room, and two bedrooms. The rooms were small, but they were all hers. She sat on the porch steps.

He stood and dragged her with him. "I haven't even shown you this. We've got a garage."

A small white building stood in the corner of the yard. "I can drive right in from the alley." Ottis opened the side door to the garage. Augusta stood in the middle of the yard. "How can we afford all this?"

"Business is going great guns. I have to run to keep up

with the people who want to give me money." He took her hand. "Don't worry, I've got this."

* * *

"What do you mean, moving?" Agata was braiding Thelma's hair.

"Ottis and I are getting married and moving into a house."

"A house, a real house—I am so happy for you." Tears welled in Agata's eyes as she continued to braid.

Augusta fought back tears. "It will be too far away for you to take care of the girls while I work."

"I know, I know, I will miss all of you." She kissed the back of Thelma's head.

There wasn't a lot to move, but Ottis borrowed a truck for the project. There were a few boxes of plates and cookware, and their clothing fit into four shopping bags. Another bag contained bits of leftover food, spices, and cleaning products.

"Be careful with that." Augusta watched Ottis carry her grandmother's rocking chair down the stairs. She turned to look at the two rooms that had been her home for too long. The table and chairs were gone. Agata said they were better than what she had, and the woman in the apartment next to hers took her old one. Edith took the small bookshelf the previous tenants had left. Augusta left the mattress on the floor, and Edith and Agata split up the pallets and bits of wood stored beneath them. Nothing goes to waste among friends.

Augusta left her dingy apartment as clean as she could. The sink and tub were spotless, the floors swept. She left a bit of soap on the shelf above the sink. Finding the soap when she'd moved in had made her first days in this tiny space a little easier. She stared out the window at the brick wall next door. She'd been fifteen and expecting her first child when she'd first walked into this room. Now she had two daughters, her husband had left, and she was remarried to a very different man.

"I thought we were done up here." Ottis stood in the doorway.

"Yes, we're done here." She closed the door on that life, ready for a new one.

Agata stood near the truck with a bag of toys. "I want the girls to keep these."

"It will make us sad to look at them," David said, his hand on his wife's shoulder.

"Wait. Wait!" Edith was running down the alley. She was catching her breath as she handed Augusta a green vase with a delicate yellow lily painted on it. "I brought this from Poland. I want you to have it for your new home."

They all cried and hugged, and David had to pull Edith and Agata back so Augusta could get in the truck. She watched them in the sideview mirror as the truck drove away.

Chapter Seventeen

Gramma's Rocking Chair

Gramma's rocking chair fit perfectly among the living room furniture in the new house. Augusta knew it belonged the first time she walked in the door. Edith's vase was displayed on the center of the dining room sideboard. Agata's toys were strewn around the girls' room, and a pair of Lincoln Log buildings had already been constructed on top of the dresser.

She'd been keeping their clothes in cardboard boxes, but they now had dressers with drawers for the few things they had to put in them. Augusta was carrying boxes to the back porch when Ottis took them from her and set them on the floor. "I forgot to show you the basement."

He led her to a door she hadn't given any attention to. He turned on the light switch, revealing a stairway leading to a room beneath the house. That space, back in Arkansas, was where her parents stored barrels of apples and potatoes, and shelves of canned fruits and vegetables. Ottis stood in the vacant room with his hands out. "Cement block construction, no stone walls. Cement throughout, no dirt floor."

Augusta had never been in a basement that didn't have a dirt floor. The cement was smooth and new, which made the monster in the center of the space stand out. She knew it was a coal furnace, but it looked like a huge black spider on its back. The spider's metal legs sprawled up toward the ceiling. Ottis beamed. "It's a state-of-the-art coal furnace, with heat ducts to every room. No more hovering near a woodstove and freezing on the other side of the room."

Ottis guided her to a corner. "This is the root cellar." The door opened on a tiny room with shelves on three walls. The entire basement of the house she'd grown up in had been a root cellar. Besides barrels of apples, potatoes, and squash, the ceiling had been hung with a variety of drying herbs. There'd been braids of garlic and onions hanging from rafters, and as winter approached, full shelves along every wall with all manner of canned fruits and vegetables. If Augusta filled every shelf in this little root cellar, it wouldn't get a family through the winter.

"Come look at this," Ottis said, closing the door. On the far wall, between two small windows tucked up against the ceiling, was something Augusta had only seen at the Sears store. Distracted, Augusta turned slowly. "Even the basement has windows on every wall."

"Yeah, but look at this." Ottis gestured toward a white cylinder that was almost as tall as she was. "This water heater will take care of us but good." Then he swung his arm toward a deep white tub on legs with wheels. Above the tub, off to the side, was a contraption with a pair of rollers. Ottis pulled the white lid off the tub. "It's an Easy Washing Machine."

Augusta could see EASY painted on the side of the tub.

Inside was a gray metal cone with a wave of edges spiraling around it. Ottis put his hand on top of the cone. "The agitator washes your clothes. You just turn it on and walk away. When you come back, the clothes are clean."

"Where does the water come from?"

"There's a set-tub right here, with two basins. You just turn on the water to whatever temperature you want, and put the hose attached to the faucet in the tub."

She walked over to look at the set-tub, but was distracted by a hole in the perfect cement floor. It was about the size and depth of the barrels they'd stored apples in back in Arkansas. Ottis followed her eyes. "That's a sump pump. If water gets in the basement, it will flow to this corner and into that hole. There's a pump in there that will pump the water outside."

Augusta thought the hole looked like something an ogre might hide in. Down in the hole, the pump did look a bit like an ogre.

Ottis was back beside the Easy Washer. "So, what do you think?"

"I—um. . . . It looks like something out of the movies."

"Yeah, this should make laundry day easier."

She didn't know if she'd ever figure out how to use the thing—there were so many dials—but she didn't want to be contrary. "Yes, it looks like it will be a lot easier." *I can figure this out, and it* will *be better*, she determined.

* * *

Augusta was basking in her new normal as she prepared her first meal on the electric stove. She'd always cooked with wood, and knew how to set the fire for a pot roast, but she had to ask Mel how to use her new stove. He showed her how he set the oven temperature at the restaurant. "Yours is gas and mine is electric," Augusta said.

Mel laughed. "Three-fifty is three-fifty. Seer your roast at five hundred degrees for ten minutes, take it out and add your potatoes, carrots, and onions, then turn it down to three-fifty for forty-five minutes, and you've got dinner."

They sat around the dining room table like a real family. The afternoon light shone through the window, and the meal looked beautiful displayed on their new table. The beef was fall-apart done and still moist. The girls jabbered about the squirrels they'd watched in the tree in the backyard.

"Can we get a swing for the tree?"

"Ivon, don't talk with your mouth full."

"I'll bring a tire and rope home tomorrow." Ottis had access to lots of old tires.

Augusta chewed quickly; she had a question. "How are you going to get up that tree without a ladder?"

She didn't want this magic to end abruptly because her husband fell out of a tree.

"I've been climbing trees all my life. We'll have a tire swing tomorrow."

* * *

"My mom has an Easy Washer. I'll come over on Saturday and show you how to use it," Jane said, trying not to laugh at Augusta's description of the strange white machine in her basement.

On Saturday, Jane turned on both knobs for the single faucet attached to the hose, and held up the loose end of it. "Just adjust the knobs until you have the water temperature you want, then set the hose in the tub. Now, what have you got to wash?"

Augusta pointed at two wicker baskets containing almost all the clothes she and her daughters owned, plus her husband's laundry.

Jane walked over to inspect them. "Good, you don't have much to wash, so it'll be easier. The first thing you do is divide them up by color. Because you're washing them by the load, you want to wash like colors together." She started arranging piles on the floor. "You should wash whites and delicates first. If you arrange things by how dirty they are, you can wash several loads in the same water, just add more hot water if it cools off too much. Wash the dirtiest clothes last."

That's how Augusta's mama had taught her to wash dishes. She could almost hear her voice: "Put the hottest water ya can stand into the dishpan. Wash glasses first, then knives an' forks, then plates an' bowls. Wash whatever's left in order of how dirty it is. The greasiest pans last."

Jane had everything divided. "Let's do the whites. We can leave the water lower, then add more for the bigger loads." She turned the water off and set the hose in the right side of the set-tub, put in the drain stopper, and turned on the cold water. "This will be your rinse water." She walked to the front of the washer, dropped the whites into the warm water, added laundry powder, turned the big knob to the number twelve, then pushed the button next to it. The agitator began rotating. "There you go. This will turn off in twelve minutes. There's enough water in the sink for rinsing," she said, turning off the water.

She set the other clothes back in the baskets. "I'm setting these back in the order you'll want to wash them. You may want to divide them upstairs before you bring them down here. This floor isn't going to stay this clean for long." She straightened up and put her hands on her hips. "How about some coffee?"

Augusta set a box of doughnuts on the table; she knew Jane loved doughnuts. She'd figured out that the stove's number four button heated up fast and hot, and the number one button was good for simmering, low and slow. They sat at the kitchen table waiting for the coffee to percolate. Augusta had coffee ready in minutes, no wood, no fire, no mess. *This is handy.*

Jane tapped the gray marbled tabletop. "Formica." She looked down at the gray chair cushion next to her. "Vinyl. You've got the latest stuff."

"Ottis said the kitchen and basement were so old and beat up, they had to remodel before they could rent it out. I like the yellow kitchen."

Jane looked around. "Yeah, it's bright and cheery." She looked at Augusta. "I was wrong about Ottis. I thought he might be a love-'em-and-leave-'em type, but here he is married and providing for you and your girls."

Halfway through their coffee and doughnuts, they heard the washing machine stop. Jane jumped up. "It's handy that the machine is right below your table—you can hear it stop."

Back in the basement, Jane took the lid off the washer and rotated the roller contraption a few inches. "I didn't ask Ottis about that," Augusta said. "It looks so strange."

"It's a mangle. The Easy Washer people call it a wringer, but most people call it a mangle. You have to be careful, or it'll mangle your hand. You arrange the mangle so the wash water gets squeezed back into the washer, then push this button." The rollers began to slowly roll against one another.

Jane picked up one of Ivon's white blouses. "The mangle will mangle buttons too, so hold the blouse up by the collar and turn it so it becomes a tube with the buttons on the inside. Then guide the collar in between the rollers."

The blouse began to glide between the rollers, coming out flat as a pancake on the other side. Augusta thought it looked like a cartoon character smashed flat by a steamroller. When the blouse was through the rollers, Jane gave the cloth pancake a couple shakes, and it was blouse again—like the cartoon stood up after being run over by the steamroller and shook itself back to normal. Jane dropped it into the rinse water and said to Augusta, "Now you try it."

Augusta pulled up one of Ottis's white shirts, held it by the collar, and folded it into a tube with the buttons inside. Jane stepped up. "Men's shirts have buttons on the cuffs too, so this is a little trickier. Put the collar through the same way, then hang onto the cuffs and turn them in toward the shirt when they get near the rollers."

Augusta worried about getting her hands too close to the mangle, but held onto the cuffs, with the buttons turned down toward the shirt. When the cuffs were about eight inches from the rollers, Jane said, "You can let go now."

When the whites were in the cold-water rinse, Jane put the next load in the washer, put the lid back on, and started the agitator. "I set this load at twenty minutes and added more water. The really dirty stuff you may want to do at thirty or forty minutes."

She rotated the mangle closer to the set-tub. "You want the rinse water to go back in here." She ran a white towel through and set it on top of the washer lid. Augusta did the rest, and as the washer lid became crowded, Jane set the clothes into a wicker basket. Jane picked up the basket and said, "Now we hang them on the clothesline. You've got lines down here for when the weather's bad."

Augusta looked up at the ropes weaving back and forth above her head.

Back at the kitchen table the coffee was cold, but the doughnuts were still good. "Thanks for showing me how to do this. I could've figured it out, but the mangle might have done some mangling."

Chapter Eighteen

Where's My Baby?

With both girls in school, Augusta could work part time. Ottis argued against it at first, saying his wife shouldn't have to work, but when Augusta told him how much she enjoyed the work he admitted a little extra cash would be all right. On one of her work days, Agata and Edith came in for lunch. The three of them laughed, cried, and hugged. During her hug with Agata, Augusta jumped back. Agata vibrated with joy as she said, "It's true, it's true. I'm getting a baby."

Jane saw the reunion and told Augusta, "It's a slow day, why don't you sit with your friends and visit? If things get busy you can jump in, but I can handle this."

"I'll pay you back, I promise."

"Yeah, yeah." Jane wiped the counter, shaking her head and smiling.

Augusta learned that Edith had moved to a nicer apartment in Brick Town.

Agata announced, "David is a foreman now, and we been saving up to buy a house. We're moving to Cork Town."

"You both moved to small towns?" Augusta said, thinking

it would be so nice to get out of the city.

Edith laughed and said, "No, Brick Town is a community within the city. The streets are made of brick."

Agata scooted forward on her chair. "Cork Town is in the city too—it is named for some place in Ireland. There are many Irish people living there. They are so hard to understand." They all laughed.

Augusta leaned toward Agata. "Guess who else is going to have another baby?"

"You are having three babies?"

They laughed and hugged and cried and talked until they ran out of words and tears.

* * *

Augusta had her third baby in a hospital. She told Ottis it wasn't necessary, but he thought that's how things were done in the civilized world. Her girls had been born at home, where Agata had been with her, held her hand, and helped with everything.

The hospital was sterile and white, and Augusta knew no one. The nurses were as sterile and white as the building. They called her Mrs. Collins and introduced her to a doctor she'd never met. Augusta didn't like him. There was only one young nurse who seemed to see *her*, not her condition. This nurse held her hand and said, "Hi, I'm Angie. You look pretty nervous. Is this your first baby?"

"I have two girls at home, but I've never been in a hospital before."

"Oh my, this must seem so strange. Not many people have babies at home anymore. You must be very brave."

"I'm not so brave. People had babies before hospitals ever existed, and they weren't brave, just normal. Farm animals have babies off in a field." She thought of Bella and wished she were back in Arkansas, or in the tenement with Agata beside her.

Angie put a bracelet around Augusta's wrist. "You look like you'd rather be having your baby in a barn."

"I would. I don't know that doctor and I don't know the nurses."

"Well, you know me." She fluffed Augusta's pillow. "I will be right here until that little one arrives."

"You look too young to be a nurse."

"I'm not a nurse, yet. I'm in nursing school, that's why my hat is different. I have to get some things ready in delivery. If you need anything, just ask for Angie. I'll be back in a few minutes."

Angie seemed to be gone forever, and Augusta's contractions were coming closer together. "So, how are you doing, Augusta?" Angie was back.

"I think I'm going to have a baby."

"I know you're going to have a baby. We need to get you to delivery."

"What's delivery?"

"That's where you go to have your baby."

"How far away is it? I may not make it."

Angie laughed. "It's right across the hall." She started to wheel Augusta's gurney. "I think you can make it that far, but this baby is coming fast."

There were lots of people in the room. The walls were white, the lights were bright, and they draped a sheet over her so she couldn't see them. They were touching and moving her and talking to each other, but not her. Angie held her hand and explained what they were doing. "You're okay, Augusta. Just squeeze my hand and push."

She screeched when the baby came, not so much from the pain, but because she didn't like where she was. If it weren't for Angie's voice and touch she might have tried to run away even then. It felt so wrong.

* * *

"Where's my baby?"

They wheeled her back to her room but the baby didn't come with her. Angie wiped the sweat from her face with a cool, damp cloth. "Your little boy is being examined. He'll be in here with you in a few minutes."

"I barely got to see him. I don't like this."

"I can tell. Do you want me to go get your husband? He can wait here with you."

Ottis was standing beside her bed when Angie handed their baby boy to Augusta. "He's just perfect. I can tell he's going to be handsome like his daddy."

Augusta peeled back the blue blanket and counted fingers and toes, over and over. Ottis beamed over them. Once Augusta was content that her baby was all right and all there, she let Ottis hold his son. When he handed the baby back, she said, "This is a bijou."

"What?" Ottis was pouring her some water.

"Our son is a tiny jewel."

"Boys can't be jewels."

"Ah, but he is."

Angie put her arms out for the baby. "I have to take him to the nursery now."

"What? He should stay here with his mama."

"The babies stay in the nursery, where they can be watched around the clock."

"I can look after him right here."

"Sorry, Augusta, the rules are that the babies stay in the nursery. He'll be brought back to you for nursing and you can have him with you much of the day, but babies spend most of their time in the nursery."

"I don't like that."

"I was pretty sure you wouldn't."

"What if he gets mixed up?"

"He has a wristband with your name, the date, and time of his birth. He won't get mixed up. Have you decided on a name?"

"His name is Julius," Ottis said.

"Oh, a noble name." She gazed at the baby as she walked toward the door. "You have quite a name to live up to, young man."

Augusta didn't sleep a wink that night. She didn't like the hospital, she didn't like the bed, she didn't like the gown she wore, but most of all she didn't like being apart from her baby.

The next morning Angie entered the room with a wheelchair. "Let's go down and get your baby together."

"I don't need a wheelchair, I can walk."

"Hospital rules. You can wait here or use this chariot."

Augusta got into the wheelchair. They wheeled around the first corner, and Angie said, "Look, your doctor's here."

Augusta put her hand to her face. Angie leaned down

and said, "Don't be embarrassed, he wouldn't recognize you unless you pulled your gown up over your head."

They laughed all the way to the nursery.

Chapter Nineteen

Homecoming

Ottis guided Augusta and the baby from the wheelchair to the car as if they were made of dandelion fluff, ready to blow away at the hint of a breeze. He glanced at her every time they hit a bump on the road home. "How are you doing?"

"We're just fine, Ottis. Neither of us is made of china."

The girls buzzed around them as they walked from the car to the house. "Oh, Mama, can I hold him?" Thelma got the first call, but Ivon was right there. "I want to hold him."

Augusta stepped through the door and stopped. She could smell fresh paint. Where the archway to the dining room had been, there was now a door. Ottis stepped in front of her and held his arm toward the closed door. "I'm making the dining room into a room for Julius. A little boy can't share a room with his sisters."

"Right now I think he should be in the crib in our room."

"I put the crib there, but when you think he's ready, he'll have a room of his own."

Thelma opened the door. "You should look in here, Mama. There's a big airplane hanging on a string from the ceiling."

"It's only balsawood, but someday he can play with it."

"Let me put this sleepy little guy down, then I'll look at his room."

Augusta had been gone for three days. She didn't understand why she couldn't come home, but hospital rules didn't make any sense to her all the way around. She wasn't sure how she felt about losing the dining room, but the table and chairs had been moved to the kitchen. The first thing she saw when she walked into what had been the dining room was the huge dime-store toy plane. The bed was new and the sideboard would be their son's dresser.

Augusta smiled and shook her head. "Ottis, I'm afraid you're going to spoil our little boy."

She stood in the kitchen looking at the dining room table. "It's a little cozy, but I like it here."

Ottis sat down. "It's a perfect fit."

"What happened to the table that was here?"

"Your friend Jane took it. She said it would fit perfect in her kitchen."

* * *

The first time Thelma held the baby, she looked down at the bundle and said, "Hey, little buddy, I'm your big sister."

Ivon stood nearby, waiting her turn. "His name is Julius, not Buddy." She thought Thelma had already held the baby far too long. When it was finally her turn, Augusta moved her son from the arms of one daughter to the other.

Ivon gazed at her baby brother. "I'm your other big sister. I'm not the baby anymore. You're the baby now."

Thelma and Ivon doted over their brother, and both called

him Buddy. Augusta fell into the habit too, but Ottis didn't like it. "His name is Julius Alton, not Buddy."

Augusta had been having trouble with such a big name for a tiny baby. "The girls just call him that because he's so little and they want him to be their buddy. It's just a nickname, he'll outgrow it."

"His middle name is Alton, they could call him Al."

Thelma sat on the sofa with the baby in her arms and looked down at her brother. "He doesn't look like an Al. I'm not sure what Als look like, but you are just a cute little Buddy."

Ottis threw up his hands. "My son is going to be Buddy all his life. Corporate presidents are not called Buddy. Julius Alton Collins, that's the name for a business leader, a corporate president, even the president of the United States. President Buddy just doesn't work."

Ivon walked into the room. "They wouldn't call him President Buddy. He'd be President Collins."

Thelma looked at her little brother. "If you're going to be president you need to do some growing." She held him up with both hands, so he was looking down at her. "President Buddy Collins. Excuse me, Mr. President, but I think you have loaded your diaper, and it's ripe." She carried him toward the bathroom saying, "My brother, President Buddy Poopypants Collins."

* * *

The girls learned to change diapers and fussed over Buddy like a new favorite toy. Augusta stayed home from work now. She had plenty to do with a new baby and two young girls in the house. The new baby put the house into turmoil, and life rotated around him. After a few days, Buddy's position as the center of the universe was secure and everything fell into place.

Augusta thought the girls would lose interest in their little brother after a few days, but they doted on him before they went to school and raced home to be the first to hold him, even if his diaper needed changing. Augusta had to adjust her grocery shopping. Ottis was making a good income, but she'd gotten used to her added salary. It hadn't been much, but it had made a difference.

Chapter Twenty

Quota

On Buddy's fourth birthday, Augusta made a big cake for the family. They didn't generally do much celebrating for birthdays. There was always a cake and something special for dinner, but there was no party and they couldn't afford gifts. Buddy blew out his four candles, and they all sat down to eat cake.

Ottis pulled a second beer out of the Frigidaire, saying, "My new boss is killing me. He set a quota system and if we don't meet our quota we get a pay cut."

Ottis rarely talked about work except when he made a big sale. Augusta had met a few of the men he worked with; the one named Les told her Ottis was the top salesman, month after month.

"Les told me you could sell snow to Eskimos. Are your sales falling, or something?"

"My sales are up, but this new boss says I have to sell more snow to more Eskimos or he'll cut my pay each time I miss the mark he pulled out of his ass. I don't know where he gets his figures, but Les quit yesterday."

Augusta leaned toward Ottis. "I think we should watch

our language around the children. Buddy tries to copy you already."

"Yeah, I know." Ottis looked at his son, cake crumbs on his chin and icing on his nose. "Careful, little man, you're getting some of that in your mouth." Ottis finished his beer and went to bed.

* * *

Ottis sat at the table filling out paperwork while Augusta prepared dinner. He'd been doing a lot of paperwork lately.

"Damn it, Buddy, put that down." Buddy dropped to a sitting position on the floor and began to cry. Ottis looked at the pencil marks on the kitchen wall and pulled a job application off the table.

"Draw on the back of this. I don't think the other side will do me any good, anyway."

Buddy rolled onto his stomach and began drawing on the paper Ottis set on the floor. "That's a good boy, draw Daddy a new job. One that will let him pay our bills. Your mama's back at work, and I never thought I'd say this, but we really need the money from her little job."

After dinner that night, Augusta asked Ottis to sit on the back porch steps with her. "You girls watch Buddy. Papa and I are going to sit outside awhile."

Augusta sat on the top step and Ottis stood, looking across the backyard. "I'm going to have another baby."

Ottis dropped to the step beside her. "Are you sure?"

"Yes, very sure."

"Jesus, woman, I thought we were done with that. Buddy's almost five years old, we weren't supposed to have any more kids."

"Thinking and doing are two different things." Augusta tugged at the hem of her skirt.

"Jesus, Mary, and Joseph, this is not what I wanted to talk to you about. I was just wondering how to tell you we may need you to work more hours. Things are going to hell in a handbasket at work. I've been looking for another job, but there doesn't seem to be much out there. The guys who quit for other jobs are making less than I am now. We're going to need to tighten our belts, girl."

He put his arm around her and she leaned her head on his shoulder. They gazed into the dusk descending around them until they heard a screech from the house. "Buddy, you can't color in my school books! Give me that crayon, right now." Ivon was quiet for a moment. "Mama!"

Augusta smiled at Ottis. "At least this is something I can fix."

She went inside, leaving Ottis staring into the developing darkness.

* * *

Ottis was drinking more. He had a beer every night now, and a little more on weekends, but even when it made him giggle and say silly things, Augusta worried. She'd seen this before.

Ottis closed the Frigidaire. "There's a dozen eggs in there—those're expensive. Can't we cut down on eggs?"

"I wanted to make a cake for Thelma's birthday, and it takes eggs. I have been cutting back."

"Can't you buy an egg or two instead of a whole dozen?"

"I'll ask Rudy at the market."

"You need to really work on this."

"I thought you had another job lined up."

"It fell through. Right now, this is the best I can do. There's nothing better out there. I'm making more than Les at that new place he moved to. Wish me luck today—if I make this deal I've been working on, it will make my month."

* * *

As Ottis hung his coat and hat near the door, Augusta could tell his day hadn't gone well, but she asked anyway. "How did that sale go?"

"Can you give a guy a minute? I just walked in."

Augusta worked on dinner, waiting for him to be ready to talk. He pulled out a beer and sat at the table. "It's so crowded in this kitchen. This table's too damned big."

He took a deep swig. "The deal fell through. That guy was just playing with me, he wasn't ready to do anything. He just wasted my time and my chances of reaching my quota." He drank his beer down and walked toward the hall. "I'm going to bed."

* * *

His job was getting worse, and Ottis took it out on everyone around him. Thelma avoided him, but Ivon started to stay away from everyone. At dinner Augusta asked Thelma, "Where's your sister?"

Thelma mumbled something about playing outside.

Ottis announced, "We're not waiting on her again. Let's

just eat. She can do without if she can't be bothered to sit at our table."

Augusta caught Thelma sneaking out the back door after dinner with a plate in her hand. "Where are you going with that?"

"Outside. I'm still hungry."

Dinner had been a little sparse. "Did you leave something for Ivon?"

"There's enough in there."

Thelma sat down on the top porch step to eat a second dinner and Augusta went back to her ironing, wondering what to make for breakfast.

When Ivon finally came home, Augusta asked, "Where have you been?"

"Betty's house." Betty lived up the street and was in the same class at school as Ivon.

"If you're going to eat dinner with your friend you should ask me first. We didn't know where you were."

The girls glanced at one another and shrugged.

"Don't give me that. If you're going to eat at your friend's house, you let me know."

Chapter Twenty-One

And the Winner Is

Augusta stayed home during the last days of her pregnancy. The girls were at school, Ottis was at work, and she made everything as ready as she could. The day was warm and she sat on a chair on the porch. A police cruiser pulled up to the curb. Jim sat behind the wheel and Ben walked up the sidewalk toward her, smiling. "How're you doing, Augusta?"

"I'm doing fine, just sitting here waiting for a baby. How're you doing, Ben?"

"We're just out doing our regular tour and thought we'd stop by and check on you." He hesitated. "We know you're alone during the day, and Jim and I were talking. We thought if you had some problem, you could turn on your porch light and we'd know to stop in."

"Do you do this for every expectant mother in your precinct?"

"No, just the ones we like most. Just promise to turn on the light if you're having trouble, and we'll all feel a little better."

"Is the whole force on this patrol?"

"Yes, ma'am. So promise to turn on the light and I'll radio your cooperation to all the cars."

"Call it out, officer."

Augusta watched the car drive off, wondering how this had come about. Then she recalled her conversation with Jane the day before. "I'll probably be having this baby alone," Augusta had said, cleaning tables after the lunch rush.

Jane was pouring salt and pepper into the collection of shakers in front of her. "What do you mean by that?"

"I mean I'll be having this baby at home, and I'll probably be alone."

"Why don't you go to a hospital like a normal person?"

"I'm better off at home. I don't like the hospital."

"Nobody likes hospitals, but having a baby by yourself is crazy."

"Women have been having babies since the beginning of time." Augusta looked up from filling the paper-napkin holders. "Besides, we can't afford the hospital." Augusta wondered if she could find that red-haired nurse, Angie, and talk to her, but didn't know her last name.

"Wouldn't it be better to have somebody with you?"

"It would be nice, but you don't always get what you want."

"Why doesn't Ottis stay home?"

"We can't afford that. Besides, what help would he be? He'd want me to be civilized and go to the hospital." Augusta stopped and grasped her belly, took a deep breath, and said, "I think this one might be in a hurry. I told Mel I'd be staying home for a few days."

Jane must have told one of the cops, and now Augusta was part of their patrol. She'd just figured that out when another car pulled up. Two women she didn't know got out and walked toward her porch. "Good morning, Mrs. Collins, I'm Jane's mom and this is my sister, Joan."

Jane's mom had red hair and bore a resemblance to her daughter, but her clothing, by contrast, was simple. She was dressed for comfort in a loose-fitting skirt and blouse in drab colors, and low-heeled shoes. "We just picked up a couple popsicles at the corner store and thought you might want one. It's a hot one today." She stood on the sidewalk, hadn't yet stepped onto the porch.

Augusta asked, "Are you just Jane's mom, or do you have a name besides that?"

"Oh, I'm sorry, my name is Joyce." She stepped up onto the porch and Augusta accepted the popsicle.

Joyce sat on the only other chair and Joan perched on the top step. Joan didn't look like her sister; her hair was almost black and she wore a floral dress and high-heeled shoes. They talked long after the popsicles were gone; Joyce had three children, two boys and a girl, and Joan had a boy and a girl, and was an emergency room nurse at Grace Hospital. Jane had spoken to them and they'd taken Augusta on as a project. Joyce would come by in the mornings after Thelma and Ivon went to school, and Joan would come in the afternoons and stay until the girls came home.

"That's a nice offer, but I don't need it. I'm just fine."

"Augusta, you can accept our help gracefully and invite us to sit with you while you wait, or you can make us sit out in the car and wonder, but we are going to be here every day until that baby comes." Joyce smiled sweetly.

"I can see where Jane gets her pushiness."

Joyce nodded to Joan, who went to the car and came back with a box a little bigger than a breadbox. She set it next to

Augusta. "This is a package the hospital offers people who insist on having their babies at home. I know you've had babies before, but it explains the whole process and there are some items that may be helpful during delivery. You can look through it later."

"I can't afford that." Augusta said, looking at the box.

"It's free to our patients."

"I'm not a patient."

"Okay, they're not free, but this one was brought back unused. I went through and made sure everything was there, but hospital policy is to not take back these packages if the seal has been broken. I thought you could use it, but if you don't want it, it'll be thrown away. That's such a waste."

"Hospitals have a lot of silly policies."

"You don't know the half of it." Joan said, pleased that Augusta was going to keep the package.

* * *

Joan was present when Augusta's water broke, and she threw up her hands. "I won!"

Augusta just stood there.

"Maybe I shouldn't tell you this, but between the restaurant and police station we created a pool to guess when your baby would come. We had to pick a date and time of day. My sister was sure you'd deliver early in the morning. That's when all her children were born. I picked Thursday afternoon." She looked a little sheepish. "I won."

"Don't count your chickens before they've hatched. This baby isn't here yet."

They talked as they prepared. Joan went to the neighbor's and called her sister. Augusta was glad to have company, and when Joyce arrived, she asked what her guess on the birth had been. "I picked early tomorrow morning, so if this baby takes its time, I could be the big winner."

"Did any of you guess whether it would be a boy or a girl?"

Joan pulled out a blood pressure cuff she just happened to have with her. "Yeah, but there was no money involved. Most of the men picked boy, most of the women picked girl."

"So, yesterday, when the woman two doors down just happened to have the whole morning to waste here . . ."

Joyce clapped her hands. "I was afraid Wednesday might have been the winner when you got so restless just before lunch."

"I was hungry."

* * *

Everyone was in a good mood when Ottis came home from work. Joan and Joyce were getting ready to leave, and the girls and Buddy were staring at their new sister. Ottis made dinner and fussed over Augusta the way he had when Buddy was born. He'd been so irritable recently; what had once been normal behavior now surprised Augusta. Even Ivon was less tense. The girls and Ottis sat down to dinner, and Augusta sat in an easy chair brought in from the living room, holding Lottie.

Augusta fell asleep happy that night; she had a healthy little girl a few feet away and her other children were safe and healthy. Mostly, she was happy about Ottis—something must have gone well at work that day. Maybe they could again be the happy family they'd once been.

Chapter Twenty-Two

Where's Ivon

"Where's Ivon?" Augusta was looking around the breakfast table. Ottis was berating Thelma for spilling milk. "Do you think this stuff is free? You shouldn't be so wasteful."

"I didn't mean it. It was an accident!" There were tears in her voice.

"Well, you shouldn't be so sloppy. You wasted half the milk."

Augusta stood in her bathrobe in the doorway and asked again, "Where's Ivon?"

"She marched through here like the Queen of the May, and left." Ottis was sopping up spilled milk. Thelma sniffled over her cereal. Buddy stood next to his mother with a piece of toast in his hand.

"Come over here, Buddy, and finish your toast. Do you want more?" Ottis had given up on calling him Julius.

Augusta sat down beside Thelma. "Where's Ivon."

Thelma looked over at Ottis. "She had to be at school early today."

"Did she eat breakfast?"

"I don't think so." She glanced at Ottis again.

"She acts like a goddamned prima donna, that girl." Ottis was buttering another piece of toast for Buddy. "Here you go, little man."

"Ottis, we talked about swearing."

"No, *you* talked about swearing. I pay the damned rent and I'm treated like shit in my own house."

Buddy was his little man and Ottis rarely said a mean word to him. But his biting words would leave the girls, even Augusta, near tears. He could find just the right word to stab his point home. He'd turned his sales charm and wit into a weapon. He was swearing all the time and thought it was funny when Buddy started doing the same.

* * *

Augusta wiped the tabletop clean and stood with an order pad in her left hand, pencil in her right. "What can I get for you ladies?"

Lottie was three days old and Augusta was back at work because Ottis said, "We need the money."

"Who's going to take care of the children? Lottie's three days old and Buddy's only five," Augusta had said.

"Thelma and Ivon can do a little something around here. Where is Ivon?" He was drunk in the middle of the week—again.

Mel was glad to have Augusta back, and allowed her work schedule to rotate around Thelma and Ivon's school hours.

Judith and Marion asked after the children often, and Marion shared stories about her two boys. "You're lucky your girls are so responsible. I can't imagine my boys taking care of anything. They can barely manage to get through an afternoon by themselves without finding trouble to get into. It's a gashed knee, a ball through a neighbor's window, dragging home a stray dog, or some other nonsense."

Judith listened and nodded. She had no children. She and her husband, Frank, had given up after years of hoping. "I'd be happy to help—I could take care of the little ones when Thelma and Ivon are in school."

"I couldn't ask you to do that. The girls are doing a good job. They treat Lottie and Buddy like their favorite dolls." Augusta's memory flashed on an image of a doll she'd dropped into the creek when she was a child, just to see if it would float. "I'll get this order to Mel and bring your coffee."

She wasn't worried about the girls at home with the little ones. They knew how to control Buddy, and Lottie was the quietest, easiest baby. She cried less than the other three had, and almost slept through the night already. But Augusta flashed on her doll again, facedown in the water, drifting away.

* * *

Patrick and Tony sat at the counter, awaiting their lunch orders. Patrick asked, "What are you doing back at work so fast?"

"We need the money. Ottis is having trouble at work."

"We saw that son of a bitch at Omalley's yesterday, drunk off his ass and making trouble, as usual. You shouldn't have to work while he's out drinking."

Tony warned her, "He's going to lose his job. You can't drink like that, be a major-league ass, and keep a job."

Two nights later, Ottis came in the back door drunk, yelling, "That Wop cop friend of yours is gonna get his! That asshole beat me up."

Ottis didn't look any more disheveled than usual. There was no dirt on him, so he hadn't fallen down. Augusta asked, "Where'd you get hit?" She didn't see blood or scrapes.

"He never laid a glove on me."

"I thought you said he beat you up."

Ottis fell against the kitchen counter. "What have you been telling those morons?"

Augusta could see he wanted to hit someone, so she kept her voice quiet, soothing. "Why don't you sit down here." She pulled out a chair and he collapsed into it, mumbling, "I'll just go down to that cop shop and show them who they're messing with . . ."

Augusta used the tone she'd learned as a child to calm a skittish cow. "You just relax a little before you go anywhere. You look tired. Are you feeling tired?"

He leaned across the table, his head drooped onto his folded arms, and was snoring in minutes.

Thank God for small wonders, she thought, and went to bed.

* * *

Two women walked into the restaurant, but not for a late lunch. They wore straight, black, mid-calf skirts, white blouses buttoned to their necks, and jackets that resembled men's suit coats—one dark blue, the other beige. They both had their hair back in tight buns, their faces drawn tight.

They spoke to Jane, then walked toward Augusta. "Mrs. Collins, may we have a word with you?"

Whatever this was about, it did not look good. Jane nodded and gestured that Augusta should take as long as she needed. As they walked toward a table, the one with coal-black hair said, "I'm Miss Andrea Carlyle and this is Miss Janet Sawyer." She gestured toward the woman with the brown hair and beige jacket. "We're with Child Services, and we're investigating some issues with your children."

The three of them sat at a table near the door to the kitchen. The woman with brown hair, Miss Sawyer, began speaking as soon as they were seated. "We've spoken to the staff at your daughter's school. Did you know they were having trouble in school?"

Augusta didn't know what business it was to these two strangers. Miss Carlyle had not one coal-black hair out of place. Augusta wondered how she could be that together at four in the afternoon. *I bet this woman doesn't sweat, ever.*

"Mrs. Collins?" Miss Sawyer had a few strands of hair loose around her face, so Augusta directed her response to her.

"I didn't realize the girls were having trouble. They haven't said anything to me."

"Mrs. Forester, Ivon's teacher, said she sent a note home." Miss Carlyle was talking now, but Augusta spoke to Miss Sawyer. "I never got a note."

"We just interviewed Thelma and Ivon at your home, and your husband was there. He'd been drinking. The girls said that happens a lot." Augusta wondered why Miss Carlyle was still talking.

"Ottis has been having some trouble recently, but he's

been a good man in the past. We're working through a rough patch. He lost his job and he's looking for work now. It's a tough time out there."

"Ivon told us she hides under the porch because she's afraid of her stepfather."

That's what she's been doing? Why didn't I look for her, talk to her? What do these women want?

"Thelma said she takes food to her sister when she hides."

Did I know that? I should have known that. Why didn't I know that?

"In light of what we found in your home, we decided to take Thelma and Ivon into custody." Miss Sawyer looked Augusta in the eye. "We couldn't leave them with your husband, in light of his condition."

"What about the other . . ." *Don't say anything about Buddy and Lottie. They didn't say anything about them. Shut up, Augusta.*

She sat up and straightened her hair. "What about the other . . . times when Ottis isn't drinking. It doesn't happen that much." *It happens too much and you know it. Do you think they're stupid?*

"The girls said they were afraid, so we've placed them in foster care. Do you have a family member to contact, someone who may be in a position to help you?"

She thought of her mama and wanted to cry, but not in front of Miss Carlyle. "I'm not sure what I can do. This is such a surprise."

Miss Carlyle handed Augusta a business card. "Give this some thought and call to let us know what course you wish to take. You may have friends or family . . ."

Can't she see I don't have anyone? Don't cry, don't cry, don't cry. "What will happen to my girls?"

Miss Sawyer touched her hand. "Give this some thought. You may have help that you just can't think of right now. Call our office tomorrow. This is my number." She held out another card. Augusta noticed a glare from Miss Carlyle as she took the second card. "You need some time to process this. Your daughters are in a safe place, and we all want that for them."

Chapter Twenty-Three

Not Summer Camp

Augusta set the envelopes on the table. Receiving two letters in one day was a rarity and she couldn't decide which to read first, but Thelma's was on top.

Dear Mama

I am sleeping in the bed you had when you lived here. It is hard and lumpy.

Gramma and Grampa are grumpy. I have to work every day. They said you did this when you lived here. Gramma says I'm lazy, Grampa says I'm soft. He says I'll get better with more work.

I'm tired.

Where's Ivon?

When can I come home? I don't like it here.

Yours Truly

Thelma

Augusta read the penciled note twice. It was written on brown paper, torn from a paper bag. The kind of bag her father brought home with penny candy inside. Thelma forgot to mention that her grampa brought her candy. Someone had taught her how to cut, fold, and paste the paper into an envelope for her letter. She imagined her papa dropping it off at the post office window at the general store.

She hesitated to open Ivon's letter. She knew her parents would be hard on Thelma, but they'd take good care of her. She didn't know what an orphanage in Columbus, Ohio, would be like. She thought of Orphan Annie as she opened the envelope. The paper was crisp and white, and Ivon had written with a fountain pen.

Dear Mama

I am living with lots of other children.
The boys live in one house the girls in the other.
We go to school and play together.
We eat together too. The food is good.
I miss you and Thelma too.
Why can't I be with her?

Sincerely
Ivon

Her daughters were alive and well, and that was the best she could hope for. Buddy was happy and Lottie was growing. Could she ask God to change Ottis back into the man he'd been when they married? Now she hated to see him walk through the door. She'd fallen in love with his happy blue eyes—those eyes had stolen her heart.

She remembered sitting on a blanket for a picnic lunch on Belle Isle, she and her girls and Ottis. He'd picked them up in his car, and the girls had giggled from the back seat—they'd never been in a car before. They'd stopped at a spot on the east side of the island, where they could sit on the grass looking across the river to Canada. Ottis had lashed baskets behind the front fenders on both sides of the car. One contained a blanket wrapped around a pouch of ice with cold drinks inside, beer for him and Coca-Cola for the girls. He'd held a beer in one hand, Coca-Cola in the other, and said, "I didn't know which you'd prefer, so I brought both." Before Augusta could answer, he handed them to her and ran off to get the other basket. They sat on the blanket and when he opened the second basket like a treasure chest and pulled out fried chicken, still warm within a linen wrap, the girls clapped. He reached in again and lifted a bowl over his head. "Coleslaw for the ladies." The next bowl he waved in an arc before them, like a magic trick. "Fruit salad, fresh and sweet." He pulled out a bag of bread rolls, declaring, "Baked fresh this morning."

They ate and laughed, played tag on the grass, and just when Augusta thought it couldn't be any nicer, he gave the girls money to buy ice cream from a nearby vendor. When they ran off, he looked into Augusta's eyes and said, "This could be our life." His blue eyes in the afternoon sun were deep and loving, and she saw a life in them that she wanted to be part of. How had those eyes become so bloodshot and sullen?

* * *

"Ottis, wake up, you're going to be late for work." The sound from under the pillow didn't have words. She pulled the pillow away. "Wake up, it's eight o'clock."

He snatched the pillow back. "I'm not going to work." The pillow was back over his face, with his arms wrapped around it.

Augusta didn't want to shout. Buddy was in the next room and Lottie was asleep in the crib in the corner. She raised her voice slightly. "I know you can hear me. It's time to get up. You've gone to work hungover before." She reached for the pillow, but he rolled over, facedown, and clasped his hands behind his head.

She put her hands on her hips. "You're acting like a child."

He rolled onto his back and dropped the pillow on the floor. "I got shit-canned yesterday. After all the years I gave to that outfit, they dropped me, just like that."

"You must have said or done something. Were you drunk?" She picked up the pillow and glanced over at Buddy, who was drawing on the paper she'd given him.

"I wasn't drunk. A little nip helps get my sales-tongue wagging. It helps me make sales. I was not drunk."

Augusta wondered how long he'd been drinking on the job. "How long do you think it will take to find work again?"

Ottis propped himself on his elbows. "You can't give a guy a break, can you? I just lost the best job I ever had, and I don't get a few hours to think through a plan. You want me to walk out the door and just march around begging for work. I need to check the want ads and organize a sales pitch. Give me a day or two. God, woman."

Augusta hugged the pillow, trying to think of what she could say that wouldn't make him mad. She gave up and asked, "Can you get out of bed to start planning. I need to do laundry, it looks like you threw up a little."

He looked down at the puddle near his elbow. "That's just drool. A lot of people drool when they sleep. A guy can't make one damn mistake around here."

She wasn't going to argue about the difference between vomit and drool. "It's laundry day." She gathered up the blanket, folded it, and set it on a chair, then began to pull off the top sheet.

Ottis threw himself out of bed, but his knees buckled and he ended up facedown on the floor. "Jesus H. Christ, look what you made me do."

He struggled to his feet and stumbled to the bathroom. Augusta gathered the bedding and dropped it in a wicker basket. She carried it through the living room, talking to the man who couldn't hear her from the bathroom. "How are we going to live on what I make? How are you going to find a job? Who's going to hire a drunk?"

"Who you talking to, Mama?" Buddy lay on the floor working on his artwork.

"I'm talking to myself. No one else will listen."

"I'll listen." Buddy stood up with a nub of crayon in his hand.

She set down the basket and cupped his face in her hands. "You would listen, wouldn't you? I hope you stay happy when you get older. Be happy, Buddy."

* * *

Mel showed Augusta the little room behind the kitchen. "You think she'll be all right in here?" He'd cleaned the tiny storage room, replacing mops and brooms with a white crib and pink blanket. Small toys swayed above the crib, suspended from strings, and pink curtains hung on the little window. Mel wiped his sweaty brow.

"She'll be just fine here." Augusta tucked Lottie into her cozy new space. "You be a good little girl."

"Jane said she'd pick up for you if Lottie gets fussy." Mel was washing his hands.

"If it were one of my other three, I'd be more worried, but Lottie's a different baby. She's not giggly the way Buddy was, but she rarely cries. Sometimes I look at her little face and wonder—she looks like she's thinking deep thoughts or sees something we can't see."

"I thought that meant she was loading her diaper. I haven't been around a baby for a long time . . ." Mel wiped his hands on the towel he kept in his back pocket. "You could bring Buddy too. He's a cute little guy."

"He's way too active." Augusta knew her son. "He'd be all over this restaurant. I think his father can handle him at home. When Ottis finds work, we'll figure something out."

Augusta knew she and Mel were sharing the same thought. *We shouldn't say "when" Ottis finds work, but "if."* He wasn't trying very hard and they both knew it. Mel had lined up two interviews for him, but Ottis never showed up.

The reactions of the restaurant regulars to a baby in the kitchen surprised her. Marion and Judith marched through the dining room, around the lunch counter, and into the kitchen, gathering up the baby to coo and play with while they ate. Lottie was constantly being fussed over.

Marion was holding Lottie when she said, "I've never seen a baby who didn't mind being passed around. She's wide awake and happy with whoever wants to hold her. Does she even cry?"

"Don't say that too loud." Augusta handed her a menu. "She has a solid pair of lungs in there."

When Augusta told her about the letters from her girls, Marion said, "They sound like the letters my boys write home from summer camp."

Augusta wished her girls were at camp, swimming and playing.

The guys from the precinct carried Lottie around the restaurant too. Tony handed the baby to Patrick, saying, "You better learn how to take care of one a these. My sister isn't gonna do all the work when your baby comes."

"I know how to hold a baby."

"Then why ya doin' it all wrong? Here, let me show ya." He cradled Lottie in his right arm, then handed her back.

Patrick held the baby like a bubble about to burst. "Whoa, this one needs a new diaper. Oh, man, how can something so cute smell like that?"

Tony put his arm around Patrick's shoulders. "Augie, is it okay with you if I show Patty here how to properly tend to this situation?" Tony guided Patrick through the kitchen, grabbing the diaper bag on his way. In the alley, they used the bench Augusta had set up for the procedure. When they were done, Tony made Patrick use a hose to rinse off the diaper and washcloth they'd used.

"Clean it up good, Patty. We don't want that smell comin'

back with us. And wring it out really good. And . . . don't forget to wash your hands before you eat."

"Why don't you do some of this?" Patrick was trying to wring out the diaper without actually touching it.

"I got two kids, I don't need the practice. Come on, man, it's not gonna bite you—wring that puppy dry."

While Patrick washed up, Tony carried Lottie to Augusta. "I just want to show ya that we didn't drop her or nothin'."

"I trust you, Tony."

"You trust me, but not her good-for-nothing father." They exchanged looks that said the conversation was over, and Lottie was ready for a nap.

*   *   *

With Ottis taking care of Buddy, Augusta could occasionally work the late shift. Mel didn't ask often, but when Sheila, the young girl who only worked the dinner shift, was ill, Augusta picked up the extra hours.

The restaurant closed at nine; it had been a long day. Augusta checked the late bus schedule and knew she'd have to wait at the bus stop, with her baby, for forty-five minutes. With everything set straight and the lights off, Augusta, Jane, and Mel walked out the back door. Jane offered to drive Augusta home.

"The bus stop's right around the corner. It'll be along soon." Augusta shifted Lottie's sleeping body and looked at the wristwatch Mel had given her last Christmas.

"It's almost ten o'clock, too late to be taking the bus, let alone with a wee baby." Mel brushed his hand through his hair, which was almost dry after his day in the hot kitchen.

"If you don't take a ride with Jane, I'll take you home. I don't want you on the bus this late."

"Fine, I'll go with Jane. It's not too far out of her way."

As they drove through the darkness it started to rain, and Augusta was doubly glad she wasn't waiting for the bus. They chatted about their day and when Sheila might be back for the dinner shift. Augusta took advantage of a quiet moment to ask, "Was Mel ever married?"

Jane seemed surprised. "Why do you ask?"

"The other day, he said something about not being around a baby for a long time. Is he divorced? Does he have children?"

Jane looked straight ahead. "He doesn't talk about it, but he was married and had a little boy. They both died in a car accident."

Augusta stared at the road ahead. "That's horrible. No wonder he doesn't talk about it."

"Worse than that, Mel was driving. I guess they slid off the road on ice. He wasn't hurt, but his wife died before the ambulance got there. His son lived for almost a month, and then . . ."

They gazed at the raindrops being pushed around by the windshield wipers.

Chapter Twenty-Four

Disappearing Act

Augusta tried to shelter Buddy, but when Ottis's car was repossessed he carried on for days. She stood at the stove, making spaghetti for her family, and heard Ottis announce from the living room, "How can I find a job without a goddamned car?"

Buddy was sitting on the chair beside him. "You can take the bus, like Mama."

"A man can't find a decent job if he arrives on a crappy bus."

"Mama says I shouldn't say 'crappy.'"

"Your mama wouldn't say crap if she had a mouth full of it."

Buddy didn't know what to say to that, so he took his cast-iron bank shaped like a lion into the kitchen to make it climb over tables, chairs, and empty cereal boxes his mother left out for him to play with.

Buddy had started swearing like his father, but Augusta couldn't correct him in front of Ottis. "Buddy, why don't you go wash your hands for dinner?" He ignored her. "Buddy, go wash your hands."

Buddy slammed his toy lion on the counter. "Aw, shit."

"Buddy, you shouldn't say words like that." It was unfair to expect a little boy *not* to imitate his father, especially when they were together all day, but she had to try.

"Why? Papa says 'shit' all the time."

"I know, but little boys aren't supposed to talk like that."

"Papa says shit is just shit and everybody shits."

Augusta knelt on the floor in front of her beautiful little boy. "There are words that adults are allowed to say that little boys are not. You'll be going to school someday an—"

"Like Tommy?" Their neighbor had just started school, and Buddy missed playing with his friend.

"Yes, like Tommy. Tommy doesn't talk like that, does he?"

"No. He said if he talked like me, his mom would wash his mouth out with soap. He said brown soap doesn't taste as bad as white soap."

"You see, little boys aren't supposed to talk like that. Now, will you please go wash your hands?"

"Aw, sh . . . sure, Mama."

* * *

Augusta went through the motions, preparing dinner and caring for her family, like a robot. She had so many problems rattling in her head, she couldn't concentrate on any one of them for long—there were things she just had to do. The children were in bed and she was sweeping the kitchen floor when Ottis announced, "I'm going down to the drugstore to buy cigarettes."

She knew he'd buy alcohol, too, and wondered where he was getting the money; she was paying the bills and buying the food. She finished sweeping and prepared for the next day's breakfast. They had no eggs—they were too expensive—and they were out of butter and low on milk, but she had bread dough rising. That would have to do. Buddy liked cereal, but if Augusta sliced a piece of toast, set it in a shallow bowl of milk, and sprinkled it with a little sugar, he was happy.

She went to bed certain Ottis had wandered off to a bar somewhere. She wondered when he'd stumble in, and where he would pass out: on the sofa, in the bathroom, or sprawled across the kitchen table. She didn't care, as long as he didn't wake the children.

When she woke the next morning, Ottis wasn't there, but this wasn't the first time. He'd been picked up before, "drunk and disorderly," and jailed overnight. Augusta worried about what to do with Buddy if Ottis wasn't back before she went to work, while she prepared breakfast for herself and her children. They were finishing up when she heard a knock at the kitchen door. Buddy slid off his chair and walked toward the door, calling, "Papa!"

Augusta could see by the shadow on the window curtain, it wasn't Ottis. She took Buddy's hand and opened the door.

It was Tony. Patrick stood behind him. Their uniforms and badges looked out of place on her back porch. "Is Ottis here?"

"No, he didn't come home last night. Is he in trouble again?"

Tony straightened his belt buckle. "Word on the street is, he got into some serious trouble last night. Mob trouble."

"What does that mean?"

Tony took off his hat and turned it in his hands. "He's made a lot of enemies, but I heard he's been messing with some local mafia enforcers."

"How do you know all of this?"

Patrick stepped forward. "Cops hear a lot out there."

"What did you hear?"

"We aren't sure." Tony put his hat back on. "That's why we came by, to see if he was here."

"Would you just tell me in plain English what you're hemming and hawing about?"

Patrick took his hat off. "We don't think he's going to be coming home."

Buddy had pulled away and was playing with his lion, marching it around the kitchen floor, making it rear up and then sliding it sideways around a table leg.

"What do you mean, not coming home?"

Tony's hat was off again. "What we heard wasn't real clear. He's either been run out of town or—worse."

"Worse. What's worse?"

"We don't know." Tony's hat was back on his head. "The fact that he's not here is not a good sign."

She held onto the doorknob like a cane—if she let go, she'd fall over.

Patrick stepped up. "Augie, do you want us to call somebody, or tell somebody, or . . ."

Or what? Ottis may be dead, then again, maybe not. He may have been run out of town, or he's passed out drunk in an alley somewhere. She thought Patrick and Tony knew more than they were saying.

Patrick touched her shoulder. "We'll go by and tell Mel what's going on. Do you want us to talk to anyone else?"

She thought of Agata and Edith, Mama, Papa, her brother Joseph. What could any of them do? Her ears were ringing as she closed the door and watched their shadows walk down the back steps.

Chapter Twenty-Five

The Girls Are Back

Augusta tended to her family, then went to work, children in tow. When Judith and Marion heard of Augusta's plight, they presented a solution. "We can take care of Buddy and Lottie in our office. We could set up a space for them until you make other plans."

"Judith, what would your boss say?" Augusta asked.

"My husband, Frank, *is* the boss, and I've already cleared it with him. We can do this until you get your feet back under you."

Augusta was getting advice and offers of help from people she hardly knew. She was overwhelmed with duties to her young children, hoping she could get her older girls back *and* keep her job. She found herself jumping at every knock on the door. Would it be Ottis or someone with news of Ottis? Her head was spinning, but she kept moving forward.

* * *

Augusta and Thelma hugged on the platform at the train station while steam puffed from the engine two cars ahead and people milled around them, looking for loved ones or marching toward the cabs lined up at the curb. "Mama, I don't know how you did all that work when you were little." Thelma stepped back, holding up her battered hands.

"My little girl was picking cotton. I hated that chore—you can't do it without bleeding." She cupped Thelma's hands in hers and kissed them. "You look like you've grown three inches."

"I'm thirteen, I don't think I grew at all. Were you still growing when you were thirteen?"

I was married to your Papa when I was thirteen. "I want your life to be better than mine."

As they walked home from the train station, Thelma shifted the paper bag she'd folded her clothes into from one arm to the other, her hairbrush laying on top.

"Gramma and Grampa are mean."

"They're not mean. Farming is hard work and they've been doing it for a long time. They're just dog-bone tired."

"Gramma made me stay up all night with her and take care of a sick cow, and when it didn't get well fast enough, Grampa shot it. Then he made me and Gramma help him drag it in with the pigs." She stepped ahead, stopped, and faced her mother. "Mama, the pigs ate it."

"They would've saved that cow if they could. She must've been old or injured, or both. Papa wouldn't have fed a sick cow to the hogs."

Thelma shifted the bag again, and Augusta reached over. "Let me take that."

"I can do this." Thelma clutched the bag with both hands.

There was a time when Thelma would have handed her

mother the bag as soon as it became uncomfortable. Her little girl might not have gained inches while she was away, but she had become more independent.

Thelma asked about Buddy and Lottie, but hesitated before asking, "Is Ivon coming home?"

"I thought she'd be back before you. They had some holdup with her ride from Columbus."

"Why did she go to Columbus and I went to Arkansas?"

Augusta's mind flashed to the day she'd sat at Mel's desk holding the heavy black receiver to her ear. She could almost see her father standing at the pay phone in Ferguson's General Store.

"Thelma's older, we'll take her."

"What about Ivon?"

"Ya been written ta us fer years. Ya told us Thelma was strong an' Ivon would catch ever' cold or cough that come down the road. We can't have that."

"But, Papa . . ."

"Ya said they had a place fer Ivon in Ohia. Maybe ya should keep the girls together an' send 'em both there. This farm ain't no place for a sickly child, it's rough enough on a healthy one."

Augusta remembered when her younger sister had caught influenza. Augusta had been sick, too, but she'd gotten better and Elizabeth hadn't. The orphanage may be a better place for Ivon, but she'd heard stories about life in an orphanage.

"They only have room for one in Columbus," she told her father.

"Then ya know what ya gotta do." He made these decisions sound easy.

"Mama, are you listening to me?" Thelma stood in front of her.

"Yes. No. I was thinking about when they took you away."

Thelma clutched her bag and moved in step next to her mother. "Let's go home."

* * *

"Mama, come see who's here! It's Ivon, she's back!" Thelma hesitated. "One of the ladies who took us is here too."

Augusta had just walked through the back door after working the lunch and early afternoon shift. She set the bag she'd been carrying on the countertop and rushed into the living room. Ivon let her mother hug her, and Augusta spoke over her shoulder. "Thank you for bringing my girl home."

"I'm always glad to return a child to their family. I do have to ask you to let us know if your husband returns. The girls have already assured me that they will call if that happens."

Augusta stood between Miss Sawyer and the girls. "I've been told he won't be coming back, and at this point I don't think I'd let him in."

Augusta had to sign paperwork, and understood she was going to be watched for a while, but she'd accept whatever conditions brought her girls home. Augusta had seen Buddy playing with Tommy next door before she came into the house, and she hoped quiet Lottie would stay that way until Miss Sawyer left.

She was ushering Miss Sawyer toward the door when

Buddy bounded into the room, blond hair bouncing as he danced from one sister to the other. Miss Sawyer smiled and said, "Who is this cute little towhead?"

"Aw, shove it up your ass, lady. Who asked you?"

Ivon clapped her hand over Buddy's mouth and ushered him toward the kitchen. Thelma held the door open and said in a stage whisper, "Buddy, you've got to stop that."

Miss Sawyer looked a bit wilted. "We didn't realize you had a son."

"Yes, Buddy's my little boy. We're working on his swearing problem."

"I don't know how we missed that in our records." Miss Sawyer wrote something in the paperwork she was holding.

"I don't know how you missed him. He's been here all along."

Should I tell her about Lottie? No. If she doesn't ask, I won't say.

Augusta was surprised when Miss Sawyer didn't ask. She knew what was expected of her in order to keep her children, and finally said it out loud. "If Ottis tries to come back, I won't allow it."

* * *

Augusta looked in the Frigidaire and was glad she had chicken for the first dinner with her daughters back home. There was enough for all four of them, but she only had two potatoes. Trying to determine how to spread the food four ways, she saw the bag she'd dropped when Thelma had shouted from the living room. One of the restaurant regulars had given her a bag bulging with squash and green beans from their garden—she had plenty for dinner. There were strawberries in the bag too, for dessert.

As the girls set the table, Augusta was relieved to feel normalcy returning. Buddy danced around his sisters, asking them where they'd been and why they went away. Augusta hadn't been able to explain to him what she barely understood herself.

Thelma shared stories about the farm and how hard it was. She began telling about the pigs, but Augusta stopped her. "Let's not talk about that while we're getting ready to eat."

Thelma continued in a stage whisper, "Gramma and Grampa acted like it was just the most normal thing in the world to feed anim—"

"Thelma, why don't you tell Ivon about the candy your grampa gave you?"

"He brought home little bags of hard candy—not my favorite, but better than nothing." Augusta had loved that candy.

After Thelma told all the stories she wanted to tell, she began questioning Ivon. "What was the orphanage like?"

"Big." Ivon ate her meal as mechanically as she answered her sister's questions.

"How many kids were there?"

Augusta corrected Thelma. "Kids are baby goats. The word is 'children.'"

"How many children were there?"

"Lots."

"Did you make any friends?"

"Some." Ivon finished her meal and sat waiting to answer whatever questions were asked.

Buddy didn't seem to care who was talking or what they were saying, he was glad his sisters were home. He had his own questioning style. "Where the hell did you guys go?"

"Watch your language, young man." Augusta smiled at Buddy's excitement while trying to figure out what to say—or not say—to Ivon. She watched as her girls washed the dishes. They looked so natural together, but she knew Ivon was holding back. She didn't know how to ease the pressure and wasn't sure she wanted to hear what would likely be aimed at her.

Chapter Twenty-Six

Blowup

The breakfast table was set with bowls, spoons, and a box of Wheaties. This would use up the last of the milk, but tomorrow was payday. Buddy looked in the sugar bowl and announced, "Mama, we need more sugar." He held it up so she could fill it from the big canister on the counter.

"That's all we've got, Buddy, so use just a little."

He looked into the sugar bowl. "There's not enough."

"You three can split it. I don't need any." Lottie started to whimper from the next room and Augusta went to her. She returned to the table holding Lottie and her bottle. Thelma and Buddy were talking, but Ivon hadn't said a word. Augusta tried to think of a question or comment to bring Ivon into the conversation, but Buddy beat her to it.

"What's the matter, Ivon, cat got your tongue?"

She carried her bowl to the sink. "Who would care, anyway?"

"Ivon, you know people care about you. You know I care." Augusta set Lottie's empty bottle on the table and shifted the baby from her left arm to her right.

"No. I. Don't. You picked Ottis over us. If you cared, you would have kept us, not him. If he hadn't walked off, I'd still be in Columbus and Thelma would be in Arkansas. How could you just let us go? How could you leave Buddy with him? How can you say you care?"

"I do care—I love you." Tears wet Augusta's cheeks.

"How would I know that, by the way you let him treat us? By the way you let him teach Buddy to swear like a little mule skinner? What have you done that would make me think you love me?"

Augusta struggled for an answer. *I should have done more. I should have seen what was going on. I should have fought for my daughters. I should have taken better care of my family.*

Ivon stood at the back door. "You don't have an answer and you never will." The screen door slammed behind her.

* * *

The afternoon sun slanted through the latticework beneath the porch. Ivon was in the far corner, arms and ankles crossed, cobwebs in her hair. It seemed appropriate that Augusta should crawl to her daughter. She got as close as she dared, not wanting Ivon to bolt. The porch floor was too low for her to sit, so she lay on her stomach with her arms crossed in front of her. "We need to talk."

"I don't want to."

"Can I ask you to listen? I know I don't deserve it, but will you just listen?"

"I'm listening."

Augusta had been thinking all day about what to say to Ivon, but everything she thought of failed to express her true feelings. "I don't know where to start, there are so many things I *could* have done, *should* have done, better. When they took you girls, I tried to think of a way to keep you. I talked to everyone I could think of. Warren, that attorney who's a regular at the restaurant, looked into it and said the only way to keep you would be to get rid of Ottis."

"Why didn't you do that? Why did you get rid of us and not him?" Ivon tightened her arms across her chest.

"I don't make enough money to take care of all of you. Warren said if Child Services found out, they might put all of you in an orphanage: you and Thelma, Buddy and Lottie—all of you. You two were older, and I was trying to make it better. My parents took Thelma because she was older and could work on the farm. You were going to go to a place in Bay City, up near the thumb of Michigan's mitten. Tony looked into it and said it wasn't the worst orphanage in the world, but he thought it was probably on the list. Patrick's sister is a nun at the orphanage in Columbus. They didn't have space, but she said she'd fit you in and look after you."

Ivon whispered, "Sister Raymond." Her arms relaxed a bit.

"I didn't know her name, Patrick just called her My Sister the Sister. Everyone I talked to said that was the best I could do. After they took you girls, I tried *not* to hate Ottis, but he didn't make it easy. I just kept hoping he'd turn back into the man I married, and there were glimmers—or maybe I imagined it. Do you remember what he was like before? I let myself fall in love with a man I thought would be good for my children. But I was wrong."

"He was nice at first, and funny. He got us this house and

we had better food and you laughed. You didn't laugh much before." Ivon's hands dropped into her lap.

"Why were you afraid of him? Did he hurt you?"

Augusta thought Ivon wasn't going to answer, but Ivon looked up and said, "When he was drinking he would touch me sometimes. Not too bad, but I knew it wasn't right. He'd run his hand back and forth on my arm or touch my cheek. Thelma said he did that to her once and she kicked him in the balls. He never touched her again. She said I should do that too, but it was easier for me to hide down here."

Augusta flashed on times when Ottis was drunk and she'd avoided him. *If I hadn't pulled away from him, he would have left my girls alone. This is my fault—all my fault.* "I didn't know about that. Why didn't you tell me?"

"I don't know. I guess I was embarrassed. If I was strong, like Thelma, I could have made him leave me alone."

"You should have told me. I would have made that stop. I could have done that for you. He never did anything . . . else, did he?"

"No, I would have kicked him good. I think."

Augusta rearranged her arms in the dusty soil; her shoulders were starting to ache. "You don't remember where we used to live."

"I remember. It was little and dark. It smelled funny and there was lots of noise. There was only one window and it looked at a brick wall. I used to hang out the window to look up at the sky."

"How can you remember that? You were so little."

"I'm older than my years. That's what Sister Raymond said."

"That's my fault too." Augusta rearranged her elbows; her

left arm was falling asleep. "Why don't we go sit in the house and talk?"

Ivon looked up at the floorboards of the porch. "Where is everyone? I haven't heard any noise up there."

"Judith and Frank are fixing dinner for Thelma and Buddy at their house, and taking care of Lottie. Mel gave me two Coca-Colas and fixings for hamburgers. We can cook dinner together and talk some more." She lifted her right shoulder, then her left. "If we don't get out of here soon, you're going to have to drag me out of here like a dead cow."

Ivon crawled toward the gap in the latticework. "That's Thelma's job, not mine."

* * *

"Why are you doing all of this?" Ivon asked as she turned the burgers.

"Doing what?" Augusta set ketchup on the table.

"This: sending everyone away and making burgers with me."

"Because you're angry and you are *so* important." Augusta set the buns on the table and went to the Frigidaire for the Coca-Colas. "I know you don't believe me, but I love you."

"So, you arranged all this for me?" She turned the burgers again. She was overcooking them, but Augusta didn't say anything.

"I wanted to try to explain what I tried to do, but it doesn't seem like much when I say it out loud."

Ivon set the burgers on a plate and brought them to the table. "Are you sorry you married my daddy?"

Augusta hadn't seen that coming. "What made you think of that?"

"Gramma told Thelma they made you get married when you were thirteen. She told her that if Thelma was her daughter and the right man came along, she'd do it again. Thelma said Gramma's mean as a snake."

How could I defend that behavior to someone who has no idea how hard her grandmother's life has been? My children will never understand. "My mama lived a hard life, and it's all she knows. Simon was a good man, with a farm that was doing well, and my mama thought he would give me a good life. She did that because she loved me."

"Like how you sent me to a better orphanage."

"It was the best I could do. I should have done more, protected you better, I should have been a better mother."

"Mama, why didn't you run away, when you were thirteen?"

"I didn't have anywhere to run. I thought running away might be worse than marrying Simon. Besides, I was so young and Simon told me I was pretty and that I was a good cook. He was my first kiss. He was old but he was nice to me, and I fell for him."

Ivon set her elbows on the table, her chin in her hands. "What happened?"

"He changed."

"Why?"

"He put most of his farm into cotton production, because cotton prices were high. But a lot of farmers did that, then there was too much cotton and the prices dropped, and he lost his farm. It had been in his family for five generations, and he lost it. He felt like a failure and he started to drink. When we moved to Detroit he stopped drinking. We would have made a life together, but he met another woman. He left with her and I never saw him again."

"Gramma told Thelma he came home with that new woman and she took one look around and left. Gramma said he followed her around like a dog and did whatever she wanted. Why didn't he do what you wanted?"

"I was just wondering the same thing."

"Are you sorry you married him?"

"No. He gave me you and Thelma, and I wouldn't trade you two for anything, even when you're mean to your mama."

Chapter Twenty-Seven

A New Normal

Miss Sawyer sat in the living room talking to the children while Augusta waited in the bedroom. Miss Sawyer felt the children would be more forthcoming if she stayed away while they talked. Buddy had been coached about his swearing. Ivon told him, "If you say one teeny-weeny little swear word, you'll end up in an orphanage or, worse, you could go live with Gramma and Grampa."

Augusta hated these inspections. She stayed in the bedroom with Lottie, hoping her quiet baby wouldn't make any noise. When the girls were done one of them would go to the bedroom and tend Lottie until The Mean Lady left. That's what the children called her, The Mean Lady.

Augusta took her position in the living room while Thelma went to the bedroom and Ivon took Buddy to the kitchen. Miss Sawyer shuffled through her papers. "Mrs. Collins, we've been looking over your financials and we have some concerns. Looking at your income and rental costs, utilities, and factoring in food, you appear to be stretched pretty thin."

"I've been making ends meet."

"What would happen if something went wrong? What if one of the children got sick or, God forbid, you became ill?"

What would happen if a bolt of lightning struck you right where you're sitting? Augusta, don't think such things, you know she may be right. "There are many things that could happen to us, good or bad. Most people don't have enough money to handle all of them. I'm healthy, I work hard, I have family and friends, and I think I'd find a way to deal with whatever comes down the road."

"That's not a very reassuring answer."

"How would *you* answer that question?" Their stare-down was broken by a baby's cry. Augusta went to the bedroom and came out carrying Lottie.

"Who is this?" Miss Sawyer looked at the bundle in Augusta's arms.

"I'm taking care of her for a friend." Augusta didn't know what else to say.

"So you're taking in children for day care?"

"No, I'm taking care of a friend's baby for a few hours. I thought people did that sort of thing for their friends." *Don't get snooty, Augusta, this woman could make big trouble for you. If you can't afford three children, having a fourth could mean losing them all.*

Thelma stepped in. "Judith leaves Lottie with us sometimes. Judith is really busy and kind of rich."

My children are lying for me. What kind of mother am I? "I just take care of Lottie once in a while. She takes care of my children sometimes too."

"Yeah, we go to Judith's sometimes."

Thelma, stop trying to help, you might say something I can't fix. "Thelma, why don't you put Lottie back in her crib?"

"*Her* crib?" Miss Sawyer was shuffling papers again.

"It's the crib I had for Buddy. When Lottie's here, it's *her* crib." *You're lying to a woman who could take your children away forever.*

"Well, I guess that's it for today. The children seem happy and healthy, and you have friends close by who have children too. These are good signs. I'll see you next month." Augusta held the door for Miss Sawyer, resisting the urge to trip her as she passed.

*   *   *

Dinner after Miss Sawyer's visit was always a relief. They knew she wouldn't visit again for weeks. Augusta steamed hot dogs in a pan of water. Mel gave her items from the restaurant that he said were about to go bad. She wondered how hot dogs could go bad, but she accepted his gifts. If he had been too generous she would have objected, but he gave her small amounts of what he called overstocks. "I bought too much of this or too many of those. It'd be a shame to throw it away."

That night they had hot dogs, and broccoli that had gone a little seedy. Augusta could see why Mel couldn't serve that. He didn't have extra hot dog buns, but gave her half a loaf of Wonder Bread he said was going stale.

"I didn't sell as much of this strawberry shortcake as I thought I would. The cakes are getting hard and these strawberries are going mushy." Sometimes she thought he overstocked on purpose, but they both knew she needed help feeding four children on nine dollars a week. Her rent was twenty dollars a month, utilities three dollars, and bus fare about a dollar fifty a month. That left her with about eleven dollars a month for everything else. The bread Mel had given her cost seven cents a loaf. Eggs cost thirty-four cents a dozen, so when Mel overstocked eggs she was glad to bring them home.

Eating their hot dogs, folded into slices of bread with a side of steamed broccoli, Augusta noticed a look passing between Thelma and Ivon. "What are you two up to?"

Thelma leaned back. "Ivon has something to ask you."

Ivon took a big bite of hot dog. They all waited.

Ivon was chewing very carefully and Thelma giggled. "Her friend Sally is going to the zoo and she wants to go with her, it costs ten cents."

Ivon finally swallowed.

"Is her whole family going?"

"Yes."

Ten cents would buy a loaf of bread and a stick of butter. Could she afford to give that up for a trip to the zoo? Ivon didn't look up from her plate. The girls had been so good about taking care of Buddy and Lottie, they deserved a reward once in a while.

"Yes, you can go to the zoo." *I hope Thelma doesn't want to go, but she deserves a reward too. Next week I'll get Thelma a couple of her favorite candy bars, a BB Bat Sucker and a Baby Ruth.*

Chapter Twenty-Eight

We Need to Talk

"We need to talk." Ivon sat at the kitchen table, hands folded in front of her. Augusta had just walked through the door after working the Saturday breakfast and lunch shifts. "Is it all right if I take off my jacket first?" She sat and folded her hands to match Ivon's. "What do we need to talk about?"

Ivon lay her hands flat on the table. "I guess I just have to say what I have to say." She took a breath. "I was listening to you talking with Judith and Frank yesterday." Augusta stiffened. "I know I shouldn't have done that, but once I started I couldn't stop. You talked about Judith adopting Lottie. You don't have enough money for all of us and Judith always wanted a baby. She said she loves Charlotte. Why does she call her Charlotte?"

"I named her Charlotte after my aunt, but I like the nickname Lottie."

"Well, anyway, Judith and Frank can afford to take care of Lottie—I like that name better. They have enough money and they've always wanted a baby, and she'd have a good life with them. She said they'd help you take care of the rest of your family too. How?"

"They would pay the rent on this house and help us if something went wrong." Augusta felt like she was talking to The Mean Lady. She looked around and asked, "Where are Thelma, Buddy, and Lottie?"

"I asked Thelma to take Buddy to the park and I just gave Lottie a bottle and put her down for a nap."

"Sister Raymond was right, you *are* older than your years."

Ivon folded her hands again. "So, what are you going to do?"

Augusta sat across from her daughter feeling like she was being questioned in a movie courtroom. "I don't feel like I have any other choice. I can let Lottie go to people I know will love and care for her, or risk losing all of you. What do you think I should do?" *I'm asking the advice of a twelve-year-old. I was a year older than Ivon when I got married, we both grew up too fast.*

"I think you know what you need to do." Ivon leaned back. "That's what Sister Raymond said when I told her I'd run away again before I would come back here to live with you."

"You ran away?"

"I was mad at you."

My daughter ran away from an orphanage because she didn't want to come home to me. What child would choose an orphanage over her own mother? What kind of mother would sell one child to feed the others? I guess that's the kind of mother I am.

* * *

"Mama, Ivon keeps hitting me." Buddy had both hands behind his head.

"Ivon, don't hit your brother." She didn't look up from chopping vegetables.

"I don't hit him very hard and I only hit him when he curses."

"Is that true, Buddy?"

"Yeah, but she hits hard sometimes."

"Buddy, she won't hit you if you don't swear. Ivon, be careful. You want to knock the *bad* words out, not all of them."

"Mama, you should have seen him yesterday. Thelma and I took him to Belle Isle and he kept saying he wanted a pony ride, over and over until Thelma's boyfriend paid for him to get a ride. They walked him around a big circle but Buddy kept saying he wanted to go faster. When the man let the pony go faster Buddy bounced around and started to swear. It was so embarrassing. The man behind us said he was hearing all the bad words he ever knew. Another man offered to pay for another ride if the pony would trot some more. Since then I've been walking around like this." She held her open right hand behind Buddy's head. "And if he swears, I give him a smack."

"Buddy, you know how to make that stop. What's this about Thelma having a boyfriend?"

* * *

The tune Augusta recognized as "Turkey in the Straw" tinkled through the air from a block away. "Mama, can we get some ice cream?"

Augusta could say yes without a qualm. The rent was paid and they had milk and eggs in the Frigidaire. She watched her children run to the corner to wait for the musical truck. She reflexively cradled the child who wasn't there. How long would she keep doing that? She blocked that out with thoughts about what her parents would think of a truck driving around ringing bells playing "Turkey in the Straw" and selling ice cream. She wondered if they'd ever get indoor plumbing.

Her three children stood on the sidewalk eating ice cream, Buddy's dripping off his elbow. "It's too da—" Ivon switched her cone to her left hand, her right hand poised behind his head. "It's too stinking hot, my ice cream is melting." He looked at Ivon. "I can say stinking, can't I? Stinking, stinking, stinking."

Thelma shook her head. "If you stopped talking and started eating, your ice cream wouldn't be all over the sidewalk."

* * *

"What are you talking about?" Mel had just found out about Judith adopting Lottie.

Augusta set her hands flat on her thighs, so they wouldn't try to hold a baby that wasn't there. "You know Judith, and you know she's always wanted children. You know I have more children than I can take care of, and I'm being watched by the social services people. They think I'm in over my head and they don't even know I have Lottie . . . had Lottie."

"How could you do that? Why didn't you talk to me? I would have helped you." He hesitated. "I would have married you." He smoothed over a black curl that had popped from behind his ear.

"As romantic as that invitation sounds, I don't think

another man is the answer. I married two good men and they turned into abusive drunks."

"So you think I'd become a drunk?"

"No, but I don't know for sure that you wouldn't. I don't want to take that chance. I wonder sometimes if I didn't do something that made them change."

"Augusta, you know that's not true."

"Do I? Would I want to take that chance with you— or anybody else?" The bell over the door rang and the lull between breakfast and lunch was over.

* * *

That night after dinner, Augusta fought sleep, thinking about Mel and what life might have been like. *He's a good man, but you know that can change. You don't love him, he doesn't love you.* Her mama's words rang in her ear. "Love ain't all it's cracked up ta be. A good man ta take care a ya is more important."

"Mama, can you wash this off?" Buddy stood in front of Augusta, ice cream dripping from both hands.

Chapter Twenty-Nine

Post-Lottie

Augusta walked past Judith's house often, hoping to see Lottie. She watched Judith and Frank walk to their door, Judith carrying the bundle that was her darling Lottie. Another day, she saw Judith and Lottie on the lawn in the backyard. Augusta crossed to the other side of the street and was relieved when Judith turned her back as she played with her daughter. They were on a blanket and Lottie was crawling around her new mother.

Augusta realized Lottie would never call her Mama, or ask her to pull a sliver from her finger. She knew she'd always think of Lottie as her daughter, but Lottie might never know her as her biological mother. Augusta wiped a tear from her cheek. *I can't come back here anymore, this is too painful.* Even as she thought it, she knew she would return, hoping to get a glimpse of the daughter who might never know her name.

* * *

The first Christmas after Ottis disappeared was a whole new

experience. Augusta had stopped reflexively holding her baby, but couldn't stop thinking about what the day would be like if Lottie were still with her. The house was warm, the coal bin full, and they had a big breakfast of French toast and bacon. She had gifts to give her children, and there was a big turkey ready to go in the oven for dinner. She was grateful she could afford to feed and care for her family—what was left of it. If Lottie were still with her, most of that would not be true.

As she made French toast she thought of Lottie. Later, as she gathered up the gift wrap, she wondered what Lottie's first Christmas might be like. Thoughts of how happy Judith and Frank were should have made her feel better, but it didn't. Basting the turkey, she wondered if Lottie was smelling the same wonderful fragrance.

Each of her children received a hat, scarf, and mittens, all bought at Kresge's Five-and-Dime. She'd also bought a toy for each of them, and Buddy was enthralled with his erector set. She wasn't sure what he was building and didn't think he knew either, but his smile each time a new section came together filled her heart.

Amid the Christmas joy, she still worried. What if something happened to Frank and they couldn't afford to help her anymore? What if one of her children got sick, or she got sick? What if the house burned down? *What-ifs* were hiding in every corner.

Buddy was picking up spools of thread with the crane he'd built, his grin chasing the what-ifs away. Augusta looked around the room at her children, each involved in their own Christmas thoughts. Ivon was reading her new Nancy Drew mystery and Thelma was sketching with her new tablet and charcoals. Her children were happy. Buddy's face interrupted her reverie, his nose inches from her own. "What did Mel give us this year?"

Augusta stood up. "I almost forgot, he did send a gift."

She set a huge wrapped box on the floor and Buddy tore into it. "Wow! Look at this."

Within the box was an ornately painted balsawood stage with a red satin curtain that opened and closed with the pull of a small white cord. Wrapped in tissue were three puppets. The girls unwrapped each one while Buddy opened and closed the curtain. Augusta returned to the kitchen to baste the turkey while her children discussed how the puppets worked and planned the show they'd put on for Mama after dinner. They were still working on their puppet show when Augusta called them to the table after pausing in the doorway to eavesdrop on their grand plans.

* * *

"What are you two shouting about?" Augusta stood in their bedroom doorway glaring at her daughters.

"We weren't shouting, we were having a discussion." Ivon was always first to respond.

Thelma folded her arms. "Ivon told me I could borrow her white sweater tonight for the spring dance and now she says I can't use it."

"It's Ivon's sweater. If she wants to loan it she can, but she can change her mind too." Augusta looked at Thelma. "I seem to recall you offering Ivon the use of a green scarf just last week, then changing your mind after she had it around her neck and was on her way out the door." Augusta stood back and looked at them. "You two made as much noise about that as you did today. I think the neighbors two doors down could hear you. With the money you make babysitting and working at the market, you've bought enough sweaters for ten girls. Thelma, find something else to wear."

Augusta turned to leave, but stopped short. "Thelma, is your arm bleeding again? You had gauze on that sore yesterday. Let me have a look." Thelma pulled her arm away. Augusta moved around to see her daughter's wound, but Thelma pulled her blouse sleeve over it. "It's nothing, Mama."

Ivon spoke up. "Come on, Thelma, show Mama what's on your arm." She looked at Augusta. "Some of the girls who are going with a guy take a needle and gouge their boyfriend's initials on their skin, then they pick the scab until it forms a scar so it will be there forever."

"Thelma?" Augusta couldn't believe what she'd just heard.

"John and I are in love and we're going to get married."

Augusta reeled. She couldn't say Thelma was too young, everyone knew Augusta had married at thirteen, but her sixteen-year-old acted like she was nine half the time.

"If you're going to get married, why do you need his initials on your arm? You'll have his name."

Thelma pushed the sleeve up, exposing the red bandage. "We can't get married until I'm seventeen and that's almost a year away."

In a year you'll be in love with someone else, little girl. "Thelma, if John loves you, he wouldn't want you to create a scar just for him. Did you ask him what he thought?" She could see by Thelma's face that this had been her idea, not John's.

"I don't want to see that bloody arm again. If you're going to do that to yourself, do not let me see it. You two straighten up this room before you go to the dance."

Augusta was three steps out the door when she heard Ivon whisper something. Thelma responded, "Sis on you, pister, you ain't so muckin futch."

"I heard that." Augusta kept walking.

Resting her hands on either side of the kitchen sink, Augusta wondered who the girls living in her house were. She'd thought having babies had been difficult and time consuming, but her teenage daughters were more exhausting than any baby.

"Don't worry, Mama, she won't marry John." Ivon stood next to her mother. "Sam, the captain of the school football team, has been making eyes at her lately and she's been batting her eyelashes right back."

"How do you know all this?"

"I pay attention."

Augusta heard Buddy walk in the back door while she peeled carrots. A minute later, she heard Ivon say, "Buddy, if you wipe that booger under the table I will scrape it off and put it on your breakfast tomorrow."

"Ivon." Augusta turned and watched Buddy wipe something on his pants. "Buddy, there's toilet paper in the bathroom."

"That's too far away." He bumped Ivon as he walked past her.

"Buddy!"

"It was an accident, Mama."

He walked toward the living room, Ivon right behind him. "That was no accident, you little creep."

Augusta stood alone in the kitchen. *Who are these children? What happened to my cute little babies?* She flashed on her last memory of Lottie, trying to talk to her as she walked past their house. She hadn't gone back, she didn't want to confuse Lottie and it was too painful to see her daughter growing up without her. She felt guilty when she realized she hadn't thought about Lottie for days. *It's been so long since I've seen her. She's three years old now—I might not recognize my own daughter. How could I not think of my daughter for days on end? What could be so important?*

"Mama, Buddy just wiped a booger on my white sweater!"

Chapter Thirty

The Garbage Truck

M el held the receiver out to Augusta from the kitchen pass-through. "It's your daughter."

"It couldn't be, we don't have a phone." She put the phone to her ear and Thelma blurted, "Buddy was playing in a cardboard box in the alley and the garbage truck ran over him the police came and they took him to the hospital and I don't know what to do."

When Augusta handed the receiver back to Mel, her hand was shaking. Mel rushed around from the kitchen. "What's wrong? What happened?"

Jim and Ben burst through the door like they were on a police raid. "Did Thelma call you? We told her to use the neighbor's phone."

"She called. How bad is Buddy?"

Jim kept talking while Ben guided her to a chair. "If the amount of noise he was making is an indicator, he's going to be just fine."

"He was crying?"

"He was screaming like a little banshee, and that's a good thing. When little ones get hurt they make noise. If I get a call where an injured kid is quiet, it means they're too hurt to cry. I hate those calls."

Ben knelt in front of her, holding her hands in his. "We can't take you to the hospital in our squad car. Tony and Patty may be in trouble for taking Buddy. We get off in an hour and we'll come back and get you. You won't get there any faster on the bus."

Mel walked around the lunch counter. "I can get you there right now." He called over his shoulder. "Jane, put the closed sign on the door and stay here until everyone finishes up and leaves."

Jane walked toward the door. "Once I close up, I'll go check in on the girls."

Mel took off his apron and smoothed his forever-messy hair. "Close up the kitchen, be sure to turn everything off, and take whatever you want for the girls' dinner." He had his jacket on, held Augusta's coat for her, and spoke over his shoulder to Jim. "You said they took him to the Children's Hospital?"

"Yeah, it's not the closest but it's the best for kids."

Ben added, "And it don't cost a fortune."

* * *

They stood in the hospital hallway, Augusta, Mel, and the doctor. The doctor was tall and lean with dark hair and dark eyes. According to his white coat, his name was Wayne. Augusta wondered whether that was his first or last name. She couldn't remember what he'd said when he introduced himself. "Your son has multiple bruises and lacerations, none of them serious. But his right femur suffered multiple fractures and we're prepping him for surgery."

"Can I see him?"

"We can let you see him in a few minutes, but he'll be sedated. I don't want you to be alarmed by that."

"I understand."

"Have you filled out the paperwork?"

"Yes, that's all done."

"Your son is one lucky seven-year-old."

Mel spoke up. "What's so lucky about being hit by a truck?"

"To have major injury to a single limb, a single bone, is rare in a case like this. And the surgeon operating on your son is one of the top orthopedic surgeons in the country."

"Kind of proud of yourself, huh?" Mel smoothed his hair.

"I'm not performing this surgery. If his injuries were to his hands, I'd be your guy. The Children's Hospital . . ." Augusta couldn't believe Mel and the doctor were having some male contest here in the hospital hallway. She heard the doctor mention the surgeon studying with a doctor named Bircher in Sweden, "renowned worldwide in pediatric orthopedics," whatever that meant. The doctor looked from Mel to Augusta. "Your son is in good hands." *Finally, something I can understand.*

Buddy looked so tiny on the gurney. Augusta knew he was sedated, but he was too quiet and she fought back panic. There were cuts and bruises on his face, but that was all she could see, and they looked pretty serious to her. She touched his hand beneath the sheet. "Buddy, how many times have I told you not to play in the empty boxes in the alley? After all those warnings, you're not getting any sympathy from me."

A nurse walked in. "We're ready for him in surgery. The waiting room is at the end of the hall."

Augusta squeezed her son's hand. "I'll be here waiting so I can bawl you out when your eyes are open."

* * *

Augusta sat alone in the waiting room. Mel had gone to get coffee, and when he came back, a man in a blue uniform was with him. Augusta thought he looked like a car mechanic. Mel said, "This guy wants to talk to you, but I'm not so sure you want to talk to him."

The man stood in front of her with his head down, like an embarrassed child nervous about having done something wrong. "I'm sorry, ma'am. I don't want to bother you, but I wanted you to know I'm real sorry about what happened."

The name Al was embroidered on his work shirt. "Why would you be sorry, Al? What did you do?"

Tears coursed down his cheeks. "I was driving the truck—the truck that ran over your boy. I'm so sorry."

He was sobbing and Augusta felt like she needed to console him instead of the other way around. "It's not your fault, Al, my son was playing inside a box. You couldn't see him, you didn't know he was there."

"Company policy. We're not supposed to run over boxes or any containers bigger than a loaf of bread. We're supposed to get out and move them. I was running late and I saw that big box and I thought it was empty and"—he paused to wipe his nose on a handkerchief—"and I was just too damned lazy to move that box." The tears began anew. "I'm just so sorry."

Augusta didn't know what to say. The man who'd run over her son wanted her to accept his apology, but she wasn't sure she could. She was worried about Buddy and her other children, and what this would do to her financially, and this man wanted her to tell him it was all right. But it wasn't all right and she didn't know how far from all right it was going to be. *What does he want me to say?*

Mel stepped in. "I guess I was right, she doesn't want to talk to you."

Al turned to walk away and Augusta cleared her throat. "Al, I can only think about my son right now." She opened her mouth as if to say more, but she didn't.

* * *

"How long do these things usually take?" The hospital was quiet and Augusta had walked into the hall to talk to a nurse. Mel was asleep on the floor in the corner of the waiting room.

The nurse seemed surprised that anyone was still there. "Give me your name. I'll check with the desk and be right back." She was back within minutes. "Your son is out of surgery, the doctor will be out to talk with you shortly."

The doctor didn't look as tall as he had six hours earlier. "Your son is in recovery and doing well." When he began to speak, Augusta realized it wasn't the same doctor. This was the surgeon who'd studied in Sweden. She was surprised he didn't have an accent. "There were four fractures to the right femur. We performed an open reduction, bringing the femur together with a state-of-the-art metal rod. He's going to be in a lot of pain, so we'll keep him sedated until tomorrow morning. You should come back to see him then."

*   *   *

Augusta stared into the night as Mel drove her home. She'd expected to be able to talk to Buddy before she left. The surgery had taken so long, she'd been afraid something had gone terribly wrong. Mel walked her to her door, and when they stepped into the living room, Jane jumped up from the sofa half asleep. "How is he?"

Mel answered, "He's doing good. I'll take you home, Jane. We all need to get some sleep." He looked at Augusta and said, "Are you going to be okay?"

"I'm good. Thanks, Mel."

"I'll be back in the morning with breakfast, and take you back to the hospital." Mel held Jane's jacket for her.

"You've already done enough, both of you. I can take the bus."

"I'll be here with breakfast." Mel folded his arms.

"I'll be here too, if Mel's making breakfast." Augusta didn't know how Jane stayed so slim, the way she liked to eat.

"You've already done enough. I can take it from here." Augusta was suddenly tired.

Mel looked at Jane. "How about eight a.m.?"

"That's good for me. Then you can get Augusta to the hospital."

Mel asked Jane, "What do you think, waffles or pancakes?"

"Waffles."

"I don't have a waffle iron." Augusta's eyelids felt heavy.

Mel said, "I'll bring mine." He looked at Jane. "Bacon or sausage?"

"Sausage—no, the girls like bacon."

Augusta opened the door. "I'm too tired to fight with you. I'll see you in the morning."

After they left, she peeked into the girls' room and watched them for a few minutes, then went to Buddy's room. *The girls are sound asleep and I should be too, as tired as I am, but I don't know if my mind will let me. I wonder if Al will be able to sleep tonight.*

Augusta lay down on Buddy's bed looking up at the ceiling. The balsawood airplane was long gone, but the nail it had hung from was still there.

Chapter Thirty-One

What Did I Tell You?

"**I** told you not to play in the boxes in the alley." The doctor said Buddy was doing well, but he was still on strong painkillers. He'd need to be in the hospital for months, not days or weeks. Recovery would be slow, and would require multiple surgeries. Even after the warning, Augusta was shocked when she saw him. She'd expected his right leg to be wrapped in plaster, but he also had bottles of liquid hanging above him with tubes running into his arm, and the bruises and cuts on his face looked worse than they had the night before. His arms, which she hadn't seen, were as battered as his face. She pulled back the blanket and looked her son over. He was cuts and bruises, head to toe.

"You can't expect sympathy when you did something you knew you weren't supposed to. Why didn't you pull the box into the yard to play with?" *I should be nicer to him—he looks miserable. But fussing over him won't make him heal faster.* "Look at all of this." She motioned to the array of flowers, balloons, boxes of candy, and piles of comics and coloring books on the counters and chairs with tags from the precinct, the restaurant staff and many of the regulars, neighbor children, and some names she didn't even recognize. The largest package contained flowers, balloons, candy, comic books, coloring books, crayons, and a View-Master, with a tag that read, "Get Well, Buddy —Al."

Augusta pored over the array of gifts. "This is too much. You should share this with other children who don't have as much."

"No, this is mine," Buddy almost howled.

Augusta held up a candy bar. "This candy would go bad before you could eat it all. I'll take some home for your sisters."

"Yeah, you can take some for them. Thelma likes the BB Bat Suckers and Ivon likes Charleston Chews. But I want the Abba-Zaba and Candy Cigarettes. Mama, you can have all the Cherry Mash, I know you like it."

Augusta dropped a Cherry Mash, BB Bat, and Charleston Chew into her purse. "That's very kind of you. I still think this is more than one little boy should have. We'll leave it all here for today, but you should think about sharing with other children. If you don't sort through it, I'll have to do it, and I might get rid of all the Abba-Zaba."

"But, it's mine."

"There are other children in this hospital who have no candy or comic books or coloring books at all. Don't you think it would be nice to share with someone who is just as sore as you are, but without a coloring book to fill the time?"

"Can I read the comics first, then give them away?"

"I suppose you could do that."

"Could you bring me a coloring book and the View-Master?"

Augusta didn't move. "What do you say?"

"Would you bring me a coloring book and the View-Master . . . please?"

"There's not enough room over there for both of them, which do you want?"

"The View-Master, please."

* * *

Augusta and the girls took the bus to the hospital almost daily. During the first few days, Augusta worried that Buddy was getting worse. He was in a lot of pain and she thought he might be getting an infection.

"We're weaning him off the pain meds," the nurse said as she adjusted the tube between Buddy's arm and the bottle hanging over his head.

Augusta followed her into the hall. "Can't he stay on the painkillers a little longer? He's so sore."

"We have to be careful with children. If they don't feel pain, they move around too much and set their recovery back. He starts physical therapy today. He'll begin moving his arms, torso, and left leg as much as his injury will allow. We can tell a lot about his pain level during the exercises. We'll adjust as needed."

When Augusta looked back into Buddy's room, he was crying. The nurse followed her gaze. "We'll give him more at night so he can sleep. Some of this pain may be because he got a new roommate last night. The boys were fast friends and I think Buddy may have wriggled around too much."

He was still crying when Augusta walked back in the room, and there was nothing she could do to help. "What are you blubbering about? A boy with candy, comic books, and toys shouldn't be crying like a baby. I brought a new Gene Autry slide for your View-Master."

* * *

Al, the garbage truck driver, kept sending candy and gifts. Augusta caught him in the hallway during Buddy's second week in the hospital. "Al, if you keep giving him candy like this he's going to weigh two hundred pounds. I know you feel bad, and I understand you want to help, but this is just too much." She pointed to the shopping bag he was carrying.

"I feel so bad about this."

"If you want to do something, bring him one candy bar and one comic book or coloring book a week. That'll give him something to look forward to, and you can check in and see how he's doing."

Al held up the bag. "What should I do with this?"

Augusta took the bag and pulled out a comic book and a pack of candy cigarettes. She handed them to Al and went to the nurse's station with the bag. "Could you please pass these out to children you think deserve or need them?" Augusta looked back at Al, who nodded his head.

"Okay, I got it."

* * *

A week later, Augusta was leaving Buddy's room as Al approached with a bag of goodies even bigger than the one from the week before. She stopped and he held up the bag. "I couldn't decide which one I should get, so I thought I'd let him pick out one candy and one comic book, then I'll give the rest to the other kids."

She walked past him shaking her head. She didn't smile until she knew he wouldn't see it.

*   *   *

A scream jangled her awake. Augusta threw the covers back, but when she got to her bedroom door she wasn't sure where it had come from. She wasn't sure she had even heard it. Had it been a dream? She looked in on Buddy, but he wasn't there. Panic gripped her until she remembered he was in the hospital.

Augusta opened the door to the girls' room. Thelma pulled the blanket up to her chin and Augusta sat on the edge of her bed. "Are you all right?"

"I had a bad dream."

"That's a nightmare. Dreams are good, nightmares are bad." Ivon sat up in her bed.

"Do you want to talk about it?" Augusta could see Thelma's face outlined in the blue-gray of the streetlight in front of the house.

"I don't know."

Ivon wrapped her arms around her knees. "I'm ready."

Thelma sat up and straightened the blankets around her. "It was weird. Our backyard was a pigpen and I had to walk through the slop and push the pigs away with a broom handle to get to the alley. Buddy was there and the garbage truck was there and the police were there. The police were going to take Buddy to the hospital but Grampa walked up, out of nowhere, and took Buddy away from Tony. Then he walked over to the fence and threw Buddy in with the pigs."

I was responsible for my daughter ending up on her grandparents' farm in Arkansas. I was working when she saw her little brother, bloody and broken in the alley. This nightmare is all my fault.

Augusta hugged Thelma. "That *was* a bad dream."

"Nightmare." Ivon couldn't leave it alone.

Chapter Thirty-Two

Merry Christmas To Me

Buddy came home from the hospital at the beginning of December, ten months after the accident. Augusta had filled out a financial report when Buddy was admitted, and throughout his stay she'd been told not to worry about the bill. She knew much of the bill would be covered by the hospital, but was certain the little things that were not covered would pile up over the weeks. The nurse handed her the final paperwork, which was pages long. There were instructions about how to take care of Buddy at home and when he needed to see the doctor again. At the bottom of the final page she found what she'd been looking for: *Amount Due: $0.00*

She showed the number to the nurse. "Is this right?"

"Yes, you owe nothing."

"Who paid it?"

"We've been telling you this hospital is a nonprofit funded by various charities and donations."

"But I thought there would be some things I had to pay for."

"Your total due is zero. It's not a mistake."

Augusta walked away thinking, *Merry Christmas to me!*

* * *

On Buddy's first day home, the girls fussed over him and he soaked it up. Thelma helped him get to the bathroom on his crutches and turned a wastebasket upside down so he could set his cast on it when he sat on the toilet.

"Yell when you're ready, and I'll help you get back to bed." Thelma closed the door as she left. She and Ivon were in the kitchen when Buddy yelled, "Thelma, will you come and wipe me?"

The girls looked at one another, then at Augusta, who was standing at the stove. "Buddy, your right leg is broken and you're left-handed. If you can't wipe yourself, I'll come in there and you won't like it."

A few minutes later he opened the bathroom door and hobbled into the kitchen on his crutches. Augusta didn't look up from the cranberry sauce she was making. "If you don't stop taking advantage of your sisters, I'll figure out some chores you can do standing on one leg."

* * *

Two days later, Al showed up at the door with another bag of goodies. Augusta opened the door, looked at the bag, and asked, "Al, what are you doing? There are no other children to give that to."

"Yeah, I know, but, um, I thought, ah, I could let Buddy pick out one candy and one comic and let your girls each pick one and then I could take the rest to the hospital, for the kids there."

The girls hovered over Buddy's bed deciding which comic book was best and which candy bar they wanted. Augusta and Al stood in the doorway, and she worried that Al was still feeling guilty about the accident, which really wasn't his fault. *Maybe I need to give him permission to stop these gifts.* "You shouldn't keep coming here every week."

"Yeah, I know. How about I come every week for a month and then . . . I think I might just go to the hospital every week. Some of those kids are in real bad shape, and their folks are poor, and . . ."

"Al, you don't have to keep paying for this accident for the rest of your life."

"I know, but I kind of like seeing the kids. Some of them don't get to smile much." He hesitated. "My girlfriend likes it too. She's waiting in the car, we're going to the hospital together."

* * *

The smell of bacon hung in the air as they exchanged Christmas gifts two weeks after Buddy's homecoming. The candles and greenery from the breakfast table now covered the coffee table near the Christmas tree. Augusta could afford a real Christmas for her children. The zero balance due at the end of Buddy's hospital stay had left her unusually flush, and she felt a rare sense of comfort.

Augusta unwrapped a small bottle of perfume and a silky scarf that she was sure her daughters had purchased at Hudson's with their babysitting money. "Thank you, girls, these are lovely."

Buddy was bouncing up and down. "My turn, my turn."

He unwrapped a wool hat and scarf from his sisters. His third gift was a shirt Augusta had purchased at Kresge's Five-and-Dime. He seemed disappointed. "You'll be glad for that shirt when you go back to school." Augusta was pleased when he pretended to be grateful and thanked her for the nice shirt.

"What's that bulge in the pocket?" She thought she might regret this part of the gift.

"Wow, it's a kazoo! A real kazoo!" He started blasting on it and the girls rolled their eyes at Augusta, wondering why she'd given him such a noisy present. They didn't know it had been free with her purchases. Its screech was louder and more grating than Augusta had expected. She hoped he'd get tired of it, or that it might break. How sturdy could it be if they were giving them away?

She gave the girls each a warm hat and scarf that she'd found at Kresge's. She could have gone to Hudson's for their gifts, but didn't think she'd ever stop worrying about money.

Augusta had warned Mel to keep his gift for the kids simple this year, and not to give her one at all. The smell of roasting turkey was beginning to fill the house, and the kazoo was set aside when the four of them sat around the Monopoly game on the floor. The kitchen table was full of dinner preparations.

"Aw, shoot." Buddy read from his card, "Go to jail, Go directly to jail, Do not pass Go, Do not collect two hundred dollars."

There was a knock at the front door. They stopped and looked at one another. Who would visit on Christmas day? When Augusta opened the door, Al stood there with a huge bag. "I know, I know, I shouldn't be here, but it's Christmas and Buddy just got home and Angie and I are on our way to the hospital with toys for the kids." Augusta recognized the woman next to him—the red-haired nurse who'd attended to her when Buddy was born.

Angie held up a pie. "We made apple pies for the hospital staff working today, and we made one for you too."

Al set the bag down. "We brought a gift for each of you." He looked at Augusta. "I messed up your whole year, let me do this for one Christmas."

Buddy got himself off the floor and onto his crutches. "Come on, Mama, Al's just being nice."

She looked at Al. "One gift only?"

"One gift."

"Let me take that pie in the kitchen." Augusta held her hands out. Angie followed her, and when they got to the kitchen, she said, "Thanks for letting us do this. It means a lot to Al. He volunteers at the hospital now. He's one of the good guys."

"You don't work at Children's Hospital, do you?" Augusta asked.

"No. Al volunteers in the children's ward at Grace, too. That's how we met." She showed Augusta her engagement ring. "We're getting married in May. I can't believe the baby I helped you with is eight years old."

Augusta was pleased that two good people had found one another, and a bit jealous of the life they would share. *I hope their marriage turns out better than my two.* "I hope you're happy together, you seem like a perfect match."

Back in the living room, Augusta found Buddy hovering over the gifts in a row on the sofa. She picked up the kazoo and slipped it into her pocket. "All right, Buddy, let's see what Al and Angie brought you."

The floor was buried in gift wrap. The girls were wearing their new sweaters, one green, the other blue. Augusta had changed into a dress that matched the hat they'd given her, and Buddy and Al were setting up his new Morse Code Telegraph Learning Set.

Watching them, Angie said, "I don't know who's more excited, Buddy or Al."

* * *

"Buddy, where are your crutches?" He'd just walked into the kitchen and was surprised by the question.

"Uh, in my bedroom, I think."

Augusta walked to the back porch, leaned over the rail and behind a bush, then leaned back with the crutches in her hand.

"Oh, yeah. I put them out there sometimes."

"Sometimes? Why would you need them? You've been walking without them for weeks. Mrs. Hunt asked me how long you were going to be using crutches. She sees you get on the bus almost every morning."

"Sometimes my leg still hurts a little." Buddy stared at his shoes.

"Mrs. Hunt has watched you fumble around with your crutches, trying to get your bus fare out of your pocket until someone else pays for you. What have you been doing with the bus fare I give you?"

She watched his mind whirl and could see his expression change when he gave up. "I buy candy."

She held up the crutches. "I'm taking these back to the hospital tomorrow."

Chapter Thirty-Three

Children Grow Up

"Mama, David and I took Buddy to Belle Isle today."

Augusta was having trouble dealing with Ivon dating. She herself had been married at thirteen, but her daughters seemed so much younger at seventeen and eighteen than she'd been at their age. "Who is David? I thought you were dating someone named Jim."

"I'm not dating anyone. We're friends."

"Make sure David and Jim know that."

Augusta was surprised every time she noticed her daughters looking like women. *How did that happen? They were babies just yesterday, and now Thelma has finished high school and is working full time as a typist for an insurance company. Ivon is in her last year of high school and has a part-time job at a supermarket.*

Augusta walked into the supermarket where Ivon worked. She preferred shopping at the old-fashioned markets, but she had to admit that being able to buy everything one needed at one store could be an advantage. Augusta was overwhelmed, however, by the size of the store. The polished tile floor reflected the glaring overhead lights.

The worn wooden floor of her favorite meat market was dimly lit. When she walked in that door, she could see Rudy at the meat counter, in the back of the store.

The supermarket ceiling was high and she couldn't see the back of the store at all. The rows of shelved products reminded her of an overgrown August garden, waiting for harvest. People bustled past as she walked back to the door. It took several visits and prodding from Ivon before she made a purchase.

Once she decided to take the plunge, Augusta stood in the checkout line watching Ivon use the electric cash register like she'd been doing it all her life. A young man moved from another checkout line and stood behind Augusta. He'd noticed how pretty Ivon was. Augusta was finding adapting to change more difficult as the changes came flying at her.

* * *

Augusta came up from the basement. "Why is there a dollhouse in the cellar?"

Ivon and Thelma looked at one another but didn't say anything. Augusta folded her arms. They looked at one another again and Thelma said, "You tell her."

"Buddy put it down there. He took it out of the Eriksons' basement."

"He stole it?" Augusta was looking around as if Buddy were hiding somewhere in the kitchen.

"Well, kind of. Jimmy told Buddy he couldn't get that big dollhouse through the Eriksons' basement window, and

Buddy said he could."

Thelma jumped in. "By the time he got it out the window, Jimmy had gone home, so Buddy had to hide it until he could show it to Jimmy, to prove he did it."

Ivon picked up the story. "Buddy showed it to Jimmy, but when they went to put it back in the basement, the window was locked."

"So Buddy left it in our basement?" Augusta's hands rested on her hips.

"He didn't know what else to do. He wanted to give it back." Ivon defended her little brother.

* * *

Buddy stood on the Erikson's front porch balancing the bulky dollhouse, waiting for someone to answer the door. Augusta stood on the sidewalk, certain he was hoping Mrs. Erikson or Shirley would answer the doorbell, but Mr. Erikson loomed over him. He looked at the dollhouse, then Buddy, then back at the dollhouse. "What is this doing here?"

Buddy glanced over his shoulder at his mother, then back at Mr. Erikson. "I'm sorry I took your dollhouse. I didn't mean to keep it."

"If you didn't mean to keep it, why did you take it?"

Buddy tapped his right foot with the toe of his left shoe, then tapped his left foot with his right toe, and the dollhouse wobbled. "I just wanted to see if I could get it out the window."

Mr. Erikson put his hands in his pockets. Augusta thought he was fighting back a smile. "If you didn't really want the dollhouse, why didn't you put it right back, once you proved you could get it out?"

"Well, Jimmy went home and I had to show him I did it, to get the baseball card he had."

"So, you did this on a bet." Mr. Erikson was laughing.

"Jimmy had a Babe Ruth and I didn't have one."

Mr. Erikson looked past Buddy to Augusta. "What do you think we should do with this young man?"

"If you have some chores for him to do, I'll make sure he does a good job."

He looked at Buddy. "The first chore is for you to take that dollhouse down to the basement where you found it. Shirley will show you the way. Your mother and I will come up with a proper punishment before you get back."

Buddy was walking down the hallway toward Mrs. Erikson when Mr. Erikson asked Augusta, "Did he get the card?"

Chapter Thirty-Four

Not a Nightmare

Augusta waited on the porch after ringing the doorbell. *Who will open the door? What will they say? What should she say?* Judith had invited her to their home, and she'd never done that before. The phone conversation had been polite and brief, conveying only key information. "Charlotte wants to meet her birth mother. Would you like to have dinner with us?"

A twelve-year-old answered the door. Her features were at once familiar and surprising. She seemed as hesitant as Augusta felt, and they looked at one another for a long moment. "Won't you come in?" Lottie stepped back and extended an inviting arm into the hallway behind her. Her blue eyes glistened, like Buddy's.

The dining room table was long and polished, and the three of them sat at one end, Judith at the head of the table, Augusta and Lottie facing each other. Augusta didn't notice what was served, she was too taken with her daughter. She told Lottie about her brother and two half-sisters. Lottie told her about school, her favorite foods, and movies she liked, then she hesitated. "I used to dream about you, about what you would look like, what you'd say to me."

"I had dreams too, but you are so much prettier than I imagined. This horse face of mine must be a disappointment." Augusta straightened her hair. "I used to walk by your house when you were tiny, hoping to see you in the yard."

Lottie's eyes brightened. "You wore a gray coat."

"You were too young to remember that . . ."

"You wore a gray coat and you wouldn't talk to me."

Augusta wiped away a tear. "That's when I stopped coming, when you tried to talk to me. I didn't want to confuse you. How can you remember that? You were so little."

"Maybe I knew you were my mother."

Judith had been quiet for so long, Augusta had almost forgotten she was there. Augusta wondered how she would have felt watching her adopted daughter getting to know her birth mother. Was Judith worried about losing Lottie? As Augusta glanced her way, Judith broke her silence. "Your mother gave you up so your father and I could have a child. We love you so much."

"I know, Mom." Lottie leaned back in her chair. "Now I have both of you. Mom calls me Charlotte, Mother calls me Lottie, and I like both names." She leaned toward Augusta. "Mom said we could all have Thanksgiving dinner here next month." She leaned back. "That is, if you want to."

"Are you sure you want my whole brood here?" Augusta looked at Judith. "My girls can eat like farmhands and Buddy never stops moving."

"Frank and I adopted Charlotte, and now I have you and all of your children to share in my life. I wish Frank had lived to see this."

"I think Dad would like us to have more family now," Lottie said.

Augusta knew Frank had passed away last spring. She'd sent a card to Judith, but stayed away because that was how their relationship had worked for over a decade. She sent cards and notes when they were appropriate, and received a paid rent receipt every month. She'd wondered if their agreement might change after Frank's death, then felt guilty for worrying about herself when Judith had just lost her husband and Lottie the only father she'd ever known. Augusta was glad for the money she'd managed to set aside, but was still relieved when the receipts kept coming.

Augusta was standing near the door putting on her coat when Lottie asked, "Could we have a family dinner together, just me and you and my brother and sisters?"

Augusta wasn't sure what to say. She glanced at Judith, but Lottie added, "It was Mom's idea. She thought it would be good for us." Lottie bounced on the balls of her feet, waiting for an answer.

"Your brother Buddy does that," said Augusta with a smile.

The evening ended with hugging and laughing, and Augusta walked home on a cloud.

* * *

Augusta was preparing dinner for all four of her children. Lottie had told her that her favorite foods were meatloaf and lemon meringue pie. *What twelve-year-old likes meatloaf? Maybe Judith makes an especially good meatloaf.* Augusta had Mel's recipe, and he had customers who made a point of coming to the restaurant on meatloaf days. But shouldn't she be making something special, roasting a turkey or leg of lamb? *She told you what she likes, and if the main course is weak, you know you make a mean lemon pie. But what if Judith has some special pie recipe?*

Augusta's dining room table had been shiny and new when it was moved into the kitchen when the dining room was made over into Buddy's bedroom. More than a decade later, it looked like Buddy had been tap dancing on it. She wondered if he actually did dance on the table when she wasn't home. . . . The tablecloth would cover that, though. She only used a tablecloth on special occasions, and for that night she'd rewashed and ironed her best white one.

We'll still be eating in the kitchen, not a fine dining room with brocade wall paper and a chandelier. Augusta stopped herself. *This is a fine kitchen, clean and well cared for, with the smell of Lottie's favorite dinner filling the air.* She needed to clean herself up before dinner and make sure Buddy didn't look like a street urchin.

She paused in the kitchen doorway. *What if my children don't get along? They don't know their own sister.* She shook her head. *This could be so awkward.*

When the doorbell chimed, dinner was nearly complete, Augusta was in a fresh dress, Buddy was playing tiddlywinks on the coffee table, and Thelma and Ivon were attempting to casually read magazines. Judith dropped Lottie off, and Augusta would take her home at the end of the evening. When Augusta opened the door, Lottie looked a little anxious, but moments later the living room was full of chatter.

Thelma and Ivon told Lottie how they used to change her

diapers and take care of her. They showed her a photograph of her as a baby, wrapped in a blanket on the very sofa they were sitting on. *How did they find that picture? I keep it in the bottom of my underwear drawer.*

Buddy looked left out. He was so young when Lottie left, he hardly remembered her. Augusta would get him into the conversation, but she had to check on the potatoes first. Augusta heard from the kitchen, Buddy had found a way to get involved. When she returned to the living room, Buddy was dancing and singing for his sisters. He had a beautiful voice and his sisters applauded as he bowed to each of them separately—such a ham.

There were few lulls in conversation over dinner. The meatloaf disappeared quickly and after dessert Lottie announced, "This is the best lemon pie I've ever tasted."

Buddy stood on his chair. "If you think this pie is good, you should taste Mama's apple pie."

"Why are you standing on your chair?" Lottie asked.

"Sometimes, it's the only way for a guy to be heard around here."

Lottie laughed until she cried, Augusta joined her, then Thelma and Ivon. Buddy sat down. "Was it something I said?"

And they started all over again.

Augusta looked around the table at her family glistening like jewels through her tears.

Author's Note

Augusta was my grandmother. She died when I was barely six years old. I have few clear memories of the woman I knew as Gramma; tiny pieces of a life that ended when I was too young to ask meaningful questions and far too young to listen. Gramma lived on a lake, and our connection had to do with sitting on the dock, watching the water, or walking in the woods. I felt a link to her that I thought traveled both ways, but I was one of many grandchildren. Did she make all of us feel special, or did I think she was so exceptional that being near her made me special by proximity? She treated children like short adults, and I liked it.

Many of the facts in this narrative are from second- and third-hand information. Through the years I've heard stories about someone I barely knew. I think I would've liked her if I'd known Gramma as an adult. I was proud when Aunt Ivon stood on my farm and said to my father, "Buddy, Mama would have loved this place."

Many of these stories came to me as comments from my parents and aunts. Some were told often, others I struggle to recall. Did she say this and do that, or did I wish she had? I cannot be certain, but the basic facts of her story are fairly accurate. Most of this book is fiction based on my grandmother's life. The names Augusta, Thelma, Ivon, Buddy, Lottie, and Ottis are accurate. Other names are pure fiction because I couldn't remember or never knew them. Some were changed because I wanted to.

Facts and contradictions:

Augusta Young was born to a hardscrabble farm family in Arkansas near the turn of the twentieth century.

"She was married off to the father of one of her classmates when she was thirteen." These are the words of her daughter, Ivon. Aunt Ivon gave me a photo of Gramma taken on her wedding day. She is not with her husband, and Aunt Ivon said, "She's wearing her eighth-grade graduation dress."

How she ended up in Detroit and ended her first marriage is unclear. I remember my mother saying that a Polish woman helped her at the end of that marriage, so I created Agata and Edith.

Facts around meeting and marrying her second husband, Ottis, are also unclear. The snippets I've heard were few and contradictory.

Thelma and Ivon were removed from the home due to abuse from Augusta's second husband. No one said what sort of abuse, and I don't remember hearing an explanation for why Thelma went to the farm in Arkansas and Ivon to the orphanage in Columbus, Ohio.

Aunt Ivon told me, "I got the better deal. I got three square meals and went to school. Thelma didn't go to school and worked until her hands bled."

I've heard that Ottis left suddenly, but also heard that Augusta was told by the authorities that Buddy would be removed from her home if Ottis remained there. That version of the story ended with Augusta dropping Ottis off somewhere in Ohio. My father looked for his father when he was a young adult, but found no evidence of his existence beyond that fateful time. My brothers, Arnie and Howard, looked for their grandfather when they grew up, but also found nothing. Howard said, "That old son of a bitch may have ended up in the Detroit River."

After Ottis left, Thelma and Ivon were returned to their mother. Augusta had four children to raise on the salary of a waitress as the Depression approached. I've also heard that Lottie had already been adopted before Ottis left.

The scene of Augusta walking past the home of the family who adopted Lottie was described to me by my mother. I imagined it occurring in the fall and I imagined a corner lot because I didn't want to think of Gramma walking in the alley. I was told there was a financial bargain struck with the adoption of Lottie, but never heard the specifics.

I remember my father telling me he'd been run over by a garbage truck while playing in an empty cardboard box in the alley. My sister, Fay, remembers being told he'd been hit by a trolley car. When he wore shorts on warm summer days, the scar from the accident and multiple surgeries was hard to miss; it ran nearly knee to hip on the outside of his right thigh. The incision scar was a half inch wide and the round suture scars on either side were an inch across, like he'd been sutured with clothesline. The surgeries were successful. There was no malformation of the leg, and my father didn't limp until well into old age.

My mother told me that Lottie asked her adoptive mother about her birth parents, and the two families merged, so I grew up with three grandmothers: my mother's mother, my father's mother, and Gram. When we went to Gram's, I had to get very close before she could see me. She was older than my other grandmothers.

Memories are fleeting and easily distorted by time and wishes. The information discrepancies I've described made it easy for me to write this book as fiction.

Acknowledgments

I would like to thank Rootstock Publishing for trusting in me again. Their editors, proofreaders, and cover and interior design people make my work shine, and they are a joy to work with. I also want to thank Joni B. Cole, at White River Writers Group, and the many brilliant writers that I have had the privilege to work with.

There were so many friends and family members who read scenes, offered helpful thoughts and listened as I thought out loud over meals and on afternoon walks: Lois Robbins, Fay Kozlowski, Lynne Cookson, Mary Drewek, and Janet Macunovich. My husband, Don, is always there with honest, productive criticism, whether I want it or not, and encouragement even when I choose not to follow his advice. He is my rock.

About the Author

Celia's first career was with horses. She trained horses and taught students on Southeast Michigan's hunter jumper circuit for more than thirty years. Her second career sent her back to school to study gardening fine arts and landscape design. Celia has kept journals and written short stories and poems all of her life. She has attended classes and writing seminars and has written articles for newsletters, local newspapers, and the League of Vermont Writers. Her first book, *Walking Home*, was published in 2021, she has been working on her craft for decades. Celia; her husband, Don; and their border collie, Flurry, divide their time between Michigan and Vermont.

 **More Fiction from Rootstock Publishing:**

All Men Glad and Wise: A Mystery by Laura C. Stevenson

Blue Desert: A Novel by Celia Jeffries

Granite Kingdom: A Novel by Eric Pope

Hawai'i Calls: A Novel by Marjorie Nelson Matthews

Horodno Burning: A Novel by Michael Freed-Thall

The Hospice Singer: A Novel by Larry Duberstein

The Inland Sea: A Mystery by Sam Clark

Intent to Commit: A Novel by Bernie Lambek

Junkyard at No Town: A Novel by J.C. Myers

Uncivil Liberties: A Novel by Bernie Lambek

Venice Beach: A Novel by William Mark Habeeb

To learn about our titles in poetry, nonfiction, and children's literature, visit our website www. rootstockpublishing.com.

CPSIA information can be obtained
at www.ICGtesting.com
Printed in the USA
BVHW081204071222
653653BV00001B/2

9 781578 691203